About the Author

Socratis E. Socratous was born in Limassol, Cyprus, in 1965. He studied Public Economics at the London School of Economics and Political Science and then worked for a few years in London as a Chartered Accountant.

On his return to Cyprus in 1992 he worked for a big banking group before starting his own firm with two friends, providing business and investment advice.

He sold off his business and was advising businesses in trouble for a few years, before assuming, in 2008, the position of Managing Director of a large private hospital in Cyprus. Since March 2014 he is running his own management consultancy firm. He is also delivering speeches and presentations to schools, businesses and other groups of people on various life elevating and management topics.

He has travelled extensively, meeting different people and cultures and has written two novels, 'The Monastery of the Fools' and 'From Alpha to Omega', as well as various articles, on social issues and lyrics.

He is married to Maria and they have two daughters, Eleni and Rafaelia.

Dedication

To my wife Maria.

To the residents, for the last fifty years, of 3 Messolonghiou Street in Limassol; my parents.

And to the three heroes of this story: Yiannis, Dionysis and Paulina.

Socratis E. Socratous

THE MONASTERY OF THE FOOLS

AUSTIN MACAULEY
PUBLISHERS LTD.

A CIP catalogue record for this title is available from the British Library.

ISBN 978 1 78455 206 0 (paperback)
ISBN 978 1 78455 208 4 (hardback)

www.austinmacauley.com

First Published (2015)
Austin Macauley Publishers Ltd.
25 Canada Square
Canary Wharf
London
E14 5LB

Printed and bound in Great Britain

Acknowledgments

The facts and persons in this book are all fictional. The ideas, however, reflect the human existence, its twists and turns and what, in the passage of time, we all know as life in its daily routine.

The monastery is also fictional, but it does exist, perhaps in diverse forms, in the hearts of each one of us. The reader has at hand a literary work in which I have laid down my thoughts and reflections on the human existence in its worldly as well as metaphysical dimension.

I thank those of my friends who have helped me put these ideas on paper. Especially Julius Markides for his advice and practical support in making this edition a possibility.
This was achieved with toil, effort and lots of solitude. I also thank those who did not believe in what I was doing, because their lack of conviction has stiffened my resolve.

Finally, I thank Maria Nicolaou Prodromou and Sophie Zachariou, who helped me with the typing and layout of this book, and Melissa Hekkers, who translated it into English. Also I sincerely thank Despina Nicolaou who has edited the original Greek version of this book with a lot of care and love. Last but by no means least; I thank all the people at Austin Macauley who did a wonderful job with this publication.

Excerpts from the Song of Solomon Old Testament

Completion of Love

He:

...How beautiful you are and how pleasing,
 my love, with your delights!
 Your stature is like that of the palm,
 and your breasts like clusters of fruit.
 I said, "I will climb the palm tree;
 I will take hold of its fruit."
May your breasts be like clusters of grapes on the vine,
 the fragrance of your breath like apples,
 and your mouth like the best wine...

She:

May the wine go straight to my beloved,
 flowing gently over lips and teeth.
 I belong to my beloved,
 and his desire is for me.
 Come, my beloved, let us go to the countryside,
 let us spend the night in the villages.
 Let us go early to the vineyards
 to see if the vines have budded,
if their blossoms have opened,
 and if the pomegranates are in bloom—
 there I will give you my love...

PART ONE

Yiannis Aidonidis

It was July, summer was at its highest peak and Yiannis's car was speeding down the highway, exhausting the road as well as the kilometres that tirelessly elapsed as time went by. It was an old car; Yiannis's financial situation didn't allow him to acquire anything better. He was trying to handle the unbearable heat by keeping the car windows down and allowing the hot air to caress his face and sweaty chest, hidden under his shirt. Usually, while driving, one of two things happens or both: you think and reflect and you listen to music.

It was late in the afternoon and although the sun was still strong, the climate had started to change. It was around that time when, often, those who live in the Mediterranean basin start to feel a peculiar euphoria. It's something I have never managed to explain, like a magical diffusion of 'things', where solutions to your problems start to appear. Magically, it's times like this that we see life on a lighter note and we let ourselves get lost in thought while listening to nostalgic ballads that express our inmost melancholic moods.

Somewhere within this galaxy, halfway between reality and dreaming, Yiannis concentrated on his driving and as the malaise of the heat slowly subsided he comfortably caught sight of a road sign. He had seen this sign on numerous occasions and had often thought about side-tracking to wherever the sign would eventually lead him: The Monastery of the Fools.

He looked down at his watch. Since he had nothing time-demanding to do and without a second thought, he let his car drift to the left. Exiting the highway he entered a provincial road. He continued following the arrows that led to his destination; driving through a village he headed towards a bigger sign that stuck out from afar, leading the way towards the monastery.

Strangely enough, each and every one of us has a different opinion about religion; church, priests and holy leaders. Despite this, when things aren't going as we hope, we all seek to hold onto something elusive, something of a higher power that we feel close to, for help. We mostly call this God, and that is precisely what Yiannis was doing at the time.

Things weren't going well for him. He had chosen a difficult path in a country where it would have been easier to establish himself if he had pursued the crowd. There were many other reasons why he could have been better off. He could have become one with the system, he could have indulged in business and chosen a sector in which there was money, regardless of whether he liked it or not or, if it corresponded to his dreams.

Yiannis was a graduate of English literature and philosophy and wanted to become a writer. He knocked on countless doors and, from time to time, wrote articles in newspapers in order to pay the bills – but that was all. He sent out drafts of his work to publishing houses, poems under pseudonyms to competitions; but something was missing and he knew it. He needed something to lift his spirits. He needed some additional inspiration. That little something that would arouse his inner self and awaken his soul and spirit. He needed to find a subject; he needed to create, to write *the* story that would lead him somewhere. And Yiannis believed in himself, he put his standards up high. In any case, he had put himself up against the whole system instead of following it. Due to the connections his father had he was offered a job in the public sector or in a bank. In his father's eyes, Yiannis would have slotted in somehow. But Yiannis didn't give in. Nor did he accept the popular and accommodating: 'accept the job and continue writing in your own free time' solution. No, he would die had he pursued this 'solution'– as do so many youngsters, who, by following the advice of their elders, cease the opportunity to dream or have dreams from a very young age and they just get by.

He reached the big black gates of the monastery which, luckily, was still open and continued driving slowly towards the yard. His decision to sidetrack, to finally visit the monastery that he had ignored on so many occasions would change his life, but not in his wildest dreams could he even begin to imagine to what extent.

Dionysis Meletakis

Dionysis's car moved along the highway counting the kilometres. It was hot and humid. Surely, the heat had started to subside a little, yet he still had the air conditioning on high in his flashy sports car. He listened to music, lost in thought, and in slow motion; he took a cigarette and lit up, inhaling the poison that made his thinking clearer.

Everything had ended that very same morning. The trial had gone through for his divorce, he had pleaded guilty, took on his responsibilities and as expected, everything was settled to his disadvantage. His wife had been extremely vindictive towards him, purveying huge doses of bitterness and revenge. All within her right of course, she couldn't handle betrayal as she saw it. Although the judge, who had seemed like a good person, 'punished' him, she had also recognised Dionysis's wish to secure his children's future, which Dionysis did from day one. She granted the biggest part of Dionysis's savings to his children and left his wife in charge of the remaining household, with some conditions of course. She also granted his wife a big part of the rest of their fortune, leaving himself with some cash, recognising that he had to start his life anew. He also had to pay a 'logical' amount of money for his children's maintenance as well as the right to see them for two days every fortnight with a week at Christmas, summer holidays or Easter.

He smiled bitterly. 'The price of sticking to your virtues is immense,' he thought. He never got along with his wife, even though they had had two beautiful children together who were now ten and eight years old, whom he loved, and who loved him equally back. Facing the danger of a big scandal, by exposing a woman with huge consequences for her and her family, he took on the burden and was obligated to lie to his wife and tell her that he had had an affair with a prostitute and that it was best that they filed for divorce and paid the consequences.

The most difficult part in this situation was explaining everything to his children. He spoke to them and clenched his teeth and soul to try to show strength. His heart broke in two. Two sets of innocent eyes tried to find logic in what their father was saying to them. Their worlds shattered and unfortunately we never know how much damage is caused in such circumstances until years after, potentially not even in a lifetime. He told them that their mother and father loved them but that they stopped loving each other as husband and wife and that's why they were separating, but that both would look after them and love them forever. The youngest son who was paying more attention to the simple words he used as opposed to his father's monologue, said:

"So you mean that we won't be a family anymore?" Dionysis, almost with tears in his eyes, tried to subside the pain, "We will be my darling, it's just that the four of us won't see each other as often as we do now."

It took just a day for Petros and Marios to grow up; they lived a life's tale in action. Things we talk about, and never believe that this could happen to us.

All these thoughts; his journey, the cigarette and the radio, that played an old tune about love, brought him, without realising, at the entrance of the Monastery of the Fools.

It was his favourite place. He meditated in this remote and serene place. The perfume of the flowers in the yard and the surrounding gardens, the lemon tree blossoms overruling all other smells, the basil and the jasmine, all filled the atmosphere. Birds wandered around like angels above the church, breaking the silence with their sweet melodies. In this small paradise, with God and Saints as witnesses, is where he met Paulina on many occasions.

Paulina Antinopoulou

One hour earlier…Paulina looked at her face in the car rear view mirror. Her eyes were swollen from crying but she felt relieved. She had been in the church of the monastery for over an hour now. It is here that she has been crying bitterly from guilt, pain and helplessness for the past couple of months. When she came round a little, she breathed the air surrounding the monastery with greediness, and for the last time before heading home.

Everything had happened so fast and the end of the story was written bitterly and shorter than expected. A last glance; a last silent goodbye and an apology for why things came about the way they did, and which unfortunately, was never said. She had gone to the Monastery of the Fools early, regardless of the heat. She felt only fools could understand her as she sat on one of the benches in the yard and surveyed the premises around her. A couple of nuns she had met there that day sat with her and talked to her. Their words were like solace to her soul. They offered her savouries with fresh cold water from the mountains. The various smells were beautiful, as were the flowers, the birds, the trembling of the candle flames lit by believers, and the soft voice of the nun in charge calling on other nuns to meet, to return from their daily duties. A nun came out of the vegetable garden, another from cleaning the abbey, another from her hagiography and another from monitoring the church. After having sat there for a while, she entered the church and, hidden in a dark corner, she continued to cry.

Paulina married at an early age. In part she had decided to get married for the sake of gaining independence from her parents, with a little enthusiasm and advice from third parties ("He is a good man and he loves you, eventually you will love him too.")

All went well at first until the rigid everyday routine, the monotony, and two children were born. Two angels that is; a girl first, Sophia, and three years later a boy named Anastasis.

The puzzle was soon completed, the circle was nearly perfect. A happy mother, a wonderful husband, no one had anything bad to say about her. And her husband worshipped her. Even so, something more was needed in order to complete the circle. The 'woman' in her was missing. The woman in her was hurting because everything was enviable, and she herself felt the void, she missed love, the big love that she had never lived.

At a time when things at home were not going well at all with her husband, she succumbed to a stranger, a sweet lover, a client from the advertising agency where she worked. At least that's what she thought, because when she realised what was really going on it was too late. When you get too close to fire you will burn. And fire had surrounded Paulina and punished her for her wish to feel like a sentimental woman. She gave her body for this cause; she became a whore as she saw it in body with tragic consequences.

The tremble was strong, but she would get through it if there were no other trembles after that. The unknown client, the seductive 'Adonis' that misled Paulina was a fraud, a monster, who, as soon as he got what he wanted and had her where he wanted her, showed his true colours. One day, in one of the lousy hotel rooms in which they usually met in private, he told her that if she wanted to gain her freedom back, she would have to become bait and seduce a very well-known client of her company. 'Adonis' and his collaborators were looking for a way to 'nail this man down' and blackmail him.

Somebody with a conflicting interest had paid them to set this whole dirty network up, in the middle of which Paulina was naively standing. She now had to flirt with a stranger, fool him and break his home for her to have mere hope that she would get out of this mess 'clean' and return to her husband and children. How naïve and weak had she been!

She put her head up. She didn't even realise how long she had been crying there until she suddenly sensed she wasn't alone. She saw a very sympathetic face looking at her, an old priest, and she was surprised. It was the first time she had come across him since this was a nun's monastery. He, on the other hand, seemed to read her thoughts, and said:

"Hello my child, I'm Father Ieroclis. Today is Friday and I came here for the evening prayers. I come from a village nearby, and I help out from time to time. That's why you see me here. But I can see that you're upset. Why are you crying, what's troubling you, do you want to talk to me about it?"

"Thank you father, but I think that I'm not ready to talk about it. So much has happened in my life recently from which I have, it seems, escaped. The wound left in my soul hasn't yet healed, and I have to learn to live with it for the sake of people I treasure the most."

"Listen to me my child, I don't mean to pressure you but I'm a spiritual person, I mean, you can confess to me. If you ever feel the need to do so, come and find me, here, early on a Friday. Do you have a spiritual father?"

No, she didn't, she wasn't the religious type. She believed that confession was something other people did, not her. She was ashamed. To reveal herself in front of a stranger, even if he *was* a priest, to tell him what she did, in every detail. No, she couldn't. She couldn't bear the thought. She felt uncomfortable and stood up; she wiped her eyes, kissed Father Ieroclis's hand and exited the church.

Almost running, she crossed the yard, through the trees and got out onto the road. She got into her car and tried to calm down before setting off. Her husband and children at home were waiting for her. Her real world was waiting for her…or maybe her false one…

PART TWO

The Book

In life, what we call a coincidence sometimes isn't. It's an encounter of stars that leads us to a meeting with our destiny.

Nothing ends; on many occasions fate weaves life towards its loom in such a clever way that it scares you. This fear also makes you look at life straight in the eye and face it, follow it while it takes you to your dreams. It was a tough and difficult road on which Paulina, Dionysis and Yiannis had found themselves.

He took the last page from the printer in his hands. He leaned back in his chair and started reading the conclusion from the beginning again. He liked it; his eyes filled with tears, not so much about the content of his words and the buoyant finale, but mostly because of the heavy load he was carrying on his shoulders. He had finished the book that he had planned for many years. A book, which he wrote with so much assiduity and love. The story of Dionysis and Paulina, exactly as it was narrated to him in the Monastery of the Fools five years ago, was becoming a book, his most concrete creation; *that* was certain. The man that had changed his life on a warm afternoon in July was the leading character in the book that he had just finished.

The names had changed; it was about Alexandros and Chloe. The story was the same though, as he remembered it, in every detail from Dionysis's 'confession' that afternoon when they met by coincidence. It was necessary, however, that he add some details in order to reshape the story into a novel.

He contemplated moment by moment all the years that had gone by. His rebirth, his first short stories that were embraced by his readers, his collaboration with a small publishing house, as well as his evolution. The publishing house grew and so did he. He became a shareholder of the publishing house and their collaboration continued smoothly. He had nothing to complain about. Then, a series of poems that had received a lot of positive criticism was published and after, his first novel. He never looked back, he had followed his dreams and they had become true.

This book was a duty, that's how he saw it, a holy duty to a person that had raised his stature and ignored his position, his money and power. With a sole weapon in hand, some beliefs and virtues, this person accepted to lose everything in order to be a correct person but also to cover up for another human being, a woman.

He was patient, his ideas matured in his head for years; he studied every detail and waited. He wanted to rise first, to succeed, to get attention, to become someone and then to write and more importantly publish his book. This time had come. He had no doubt about its success.

He had already booked an appointment for the following day with his friend and publisher, Minas Damanakaki and friend Stella Papademetriotou who would help him, as always, with some good ideas and with the editing and form of the book.

Suddenly he interrupted his thoughts; he stood up, went to his balcony and lit a cigarette. There was something bothering him; he had never found out what had become of Dionysis.

Their encounter that afternoon at the monastery was their first and their last. And then, respectful of his promise to Dionysis, he never told anyone about what he had heard that afternoon. He never looked for Paulina or Dionysis. 'How strange life is,' he contemplated. 'I met a man in some monastery; he changed my life and our paths never crossed again.'

What bothered him the most was that he would publish a book that told the story about a man, and *that* man didn't even know there would be a book about him. How much he wanted to see him again! Who knows, they could have become friends. He wanted to have a coffee with him and talk about anything, he wanted them to get to know each other better, exchange opinions, walk together, talk about things that two friends could talk about...about anything.

Stella walked in and out of the office with her eyes swollen from her lack of sleep, smoking and maybe from crying too as she waited for Yiannis restlessly. When she saw him she jumped up and hugged him.

"Thank you, thank you so much," she said, "thank you for giving me the honour of reading it first. Yianni, it's wonderful, its human, well written, this book is certainly yours."

He was surprised and blushed a little, he was boiling from anxiety, deep inside he wanted to know, he wanted to hear criticism, fair comments.

"You're over-reacting," he said, "I know that it's good, I think it's the best thing I've written up to now. But I worked on it a lot and I feel I'm somehow biased. Important things may have escaped me; details, the connection of events."

She hugged him with affection, she looked him in the eyes and with her most serious expression she said:

"Yianni, I know you quite well, I believed in you; at times we came closer to each other and I think you allowed me to see things in you that no one else can identify. But last night I found out that I was wrong. What I know about you was only the tip of the iceberg, which I would say is not an iceberg but a volcano. This book, for me, who knows you better, is your own soul in a coded form.

"Within these pages I learned things that I didn't even realise existed and because you deposited your soul, and every soul in this world is unique, your book is unique. The story is nice, it flows, and it's simple. I don't know if you are referring to true events, or to people you have met or not but that doesn't matter. What I know, and believe me many people believe that what I have to say in my field of work can be considered as scripture, is that here we have material for success. We need to handle it as suits it, with respect and compassion in order to finally make a book out of it. We will not change it, we won't add or take away anything to give it more logic or take away from its character, its uniqueness. We will simply handle it as we would handle a child. We will look after it, we will dress it warmly, we will help it walk, and we will play with it. And then, where we think we are the only ones supporting it, it will reciprocate its magic, its charm. All these thoughts and feelings you have written down within these pages will come alive, will take flesh and blood and, like the bow of Cupid, it will start to warm the hearts of the people who read the book. They will be embraced by an elixir of truth, the nectar of the soul. They will read it and they'll discover their realities, their own selves."

She stopped and took a deep breath. She was out of breath and looked at him seriously.

"Yianni, this book is good and we must treat it as it deserves, starting from now."

Yiannis nodded in approval. In front of him stood a professional who spoke about his work with more passion than he himself.

Stella seemed to have composed all her energy to say what she had and collapsed on the sofa. Yiannis headed towards the window, lit a cigarette and looked out, hiding a tear that was ready to overflow from his right eye. In the background he heard Stella call Mr Damanakaki, setting up a meeting for that very same night between the three of them in a pizzeria in Kolonaki…They had a lot to discuss and even more to do.

The Success

The success of the book was beyond every expectation. The public loved it instantly, the publishing house did a good job, everyone worked collectively and the work that came out of this was something beautiful.

Yiannis gained admiration and love from the public and what honoured him the most was the respect of his colleagues. The critics of his work were brilliant and the Association of Literature and Poetry had given him the award for best novel of the year. The sales were higher than usual. Never had one of his works reached such a standard. The climax was that a foreign publishing house had asked to publish his book in English and to promote it in two other countries.

Yiannis remained humble and grounded, that was his secret anyhow. He was condescending with nobody and he ignored nobody; he never let things get to his head. On many occasions, you could find him sitting for hours talking with the old custodian of the building where the publishing house was. At other times, you could see him discussing things with the scratch-card seller. Sometimes he would go to a specific square where he knew of a shoe-shiner who spent time there. He would sit and talk to him while having his shoes polished. They soon became friends and talked for hours.

No one knew what they talked about. Suddenly, however, a series of poems would appear out of nowhere, a short story, an article and everyone wondered from where he drew his stories. It was expected, by those who knew and watched him, that he drew his inspiration from his affinity with the world and all sorts of peoples.

"Everybody has a story, something to tell us and teach us," he would often say and smile. He smiled contently about who he was, about his perseverance, about his insistence and his ideas that never failed to reward him.

Yiannis continued writing articles now that he had more exposure. His articles meant something and were followed. Yiannis Aidonidis could not send an article to a newspaper and be ignored. The themes he chose were mostly social, witty or accusations for negative associations of the system. Whether it was a scandal, an incident or something important he grasped the opportunity and wrote about it. He considered it his duty towards society and his fellow human beings, seeing as he would never become a politician. He didn't have the patience nor could he lie and do favours. Of course, slowly-slowly he realised that a man can do much more than he could ever imagine.

This was Yiannis, or almost. We forgot to mention the two persons he had in his life, or three. The one we have already mentioned. It was his friend, older by age, Stella Papademetriotou who supported him even when no one knew him. She was divorced. Marriage was not for her. She had a twenty-two-year-old daughter, a speech therapist, with whom she maintained more of a friendship rather than a mother-daughter relationship. Her relationship with her ex-husband was also friendly. Stella was a good person and was valued in her field. She got close to Yiannis at an early stage and a rare friendship evolved, which bonded them. Their friendship had passed between the sheets even though she was twelve years older than him, but when this happens and the friendship remains, nothing can break it.

The other person in his life was his brother, Alkis, three years younger than him; a musician who lived in Athens, where he studied. He was coming close to finishing his studies and was working in a nightclub with live Greek music to cover his expenses. His dream was to get into an orchestra; he played the flute and maybe one day would accomplish his dream. Up to here everything well, nothing peculiar, two brothers, Yiannis and Alkis, who lived in Athens, were very close to each other and who each had their personal life. A common story. Alkis was a homosexual; however, it was something that only Yiannis knew about in the family and that others potentially also knew through whispers.

Their parents, especially their mother, knew it; she was a mother after all, but she never said anything. Alkis, through his difference, had chosen silence. He fought alone, he created his own defences, his own world, and moved along with dignity. When he chose to speak, he spoke to his brother, Yiannis. When you confirm something that you already know, or at least you sense it, then you find yourself face to face with reality.

Yiannis was open-minded; he stood by his brother, they spoke, and he sat down and listened to Alkis's feelings with sympathy. He accepted him as he was, no complaints, nothing problematic.

"You're human, I'm human," he said, "and a good person too. I'll always be by your side," he comforted him, "and I can understand the loneliness, the distress and the battle that you have to fight in a society that's biased while living with people that don't accept you. That's why you have to make sure that you're always decent. From there on it's your right to fall in love with whoever you want and however you want."

As brothers, they were really close and Alkis owed a lot to Yiannis because he supported him and helped him. Yiannis also owed a lot to his brother. Alkis had introduced him to his muse, Erato. Erato was a bright pearl in Yiannis's life. With her we conclude to the third person in Yiannis's life.

Their story was not unusual but at the same time it was special for them. They met and got close very quickly. Erato played the violin and was a very good friend of Alkis. They fell in love and lived together. Nothing cloudy in their relationship, as everything was based in honesty and trust ; it was a normal story that probably would have had a happy ending, if we consider marriage and children as a happy ending or the beginning of a lifetime which is more stable, with different joys. At the moment he wasn't in a rush.

'Really,' he thought as he returned to the present, 'my relationship with Erato is different from Dionysis's relationship with Paulina.' In their case a scenario was written which marked the protagonists deeply. History was being written and acted simultaneously, but also abstained from being perfect.

Sitting in his armchair in his office, on the third floor of an apartment building on Skoufa Street, in which his publishing house was located, Yiannis had his back turned to the door as he scanned the view from his window. The apartment blocks opposite, the cars, the people, the signs of lawyers, doctors and other professions that advertised themselves. All crammed in small offices, concentrated on their notes with two telephones in hand trying to work.

He liked watching people sometimes, their actions, their faces. He had met Milto coincidently; a drunkard who perched on the pavement opposite, between the setback of two buildings, and who drank and daydreamed permanently. Lost in another world, with no business meetings, no stress, no telephone. He had made sure to meet him a long time ago and on many occasions he would stop at the corner of the street and speak to him. He bought him a beer from time to time or gave him money. On a couple of occasions he tried to help him by other means and Miltos got angry and Yiannis respected that. He had even written a short story about Miltos, his drunkard friend.

A wise drunkard with his own story, which we cannot reveal since Yiannis promised not to. He was watching him now, sitting on the pavement about twenty metres further down on the opposite side of the street, daydreaming with his blank and placid look, watching people walk by and smiling.

Yes, Miltos had his own story as Dionysis and Paulina did. Yiannis's thoughts abruptly turned to them. What were they doing, where were they?

His secretary interrupted him as she walked into the office without him noticing. "You're daydreaming again!" she said. She was much older than him and though she liked to keep her distance she was comfortable with him. He had given her the right to feel this way; he had a soft spot for her.

"Yes, I was thinking of something; I was thinking about two people I love." He was referring to Dionysis and Paulina as people he loved, whom he didn't really know.

"Yiannis," continued Mrs Lia, "we have to give an answer to the people of the advertising agency '*Protia*' who have invited you to accept an award for your most recent book. Of course they want you for promotional purposes too as the publishing house who is interested in publishing your new book in the UK and Ireland has given them the project to promote."

"When is the event planned for?"

"On the 2nd of November, a Wednesday night, in six weeks exactly."

"Well thank them and accept the invitation. We don't ignore anyone. I will have returned from my holidays by then and it's a good opportunity to be present at this party. Their central offices are in Nicosia, so I'll combine it with spending the weekend with my parents and friends."

When Yiannis accepted the invitation, besides the many obligations that he had, he couldn't have imagined that, exactly like six years ago when he turned left towards the Monastery of the Fools, his decision would once again change his life forever.

The Salvation

She woke up with a sweet taste in her mouth. It took her a couple of minutes to realise where she was but abruptly she managed to return to reality. She could see Dionysis hugging her tight in his arms and they were surrounded by a white cloud, the only white cloud in a clear sky. From time to time, the moon was hidden behind the cloud and lit up only the two of them who remained embraced, holding each other tight so as not to lose each other.

'What a shame,' she thought bitterly; her dream had got away once again. Reality was something else. Different. Paulina remained lying down like this for a while, looking at the ceiling. In the white background, now wide awake, she saw the last six years of her life flash by her. Difficult years, years of penitence, years filled with events, both good and bad.

Dionysis had saved her then. He had protected her from being condemned by people, from the sneer and the scorn of her family. She herself was a wreck. However, she felt that her soul had been saved. This man, this stranger, who a few months earlier was a mere client of the company she was working for, had become her shield for blackmail. Her ill-considered frivolity; not only did it not ruin her but it generously offered her what she had been seeking for her entire life. The love, as she perceived it, the sweetness of his words, the saviour of her soul, the hope, the faith in herself.

She returned to her husband and children and she really tried, she gave everything. She didn't care anymore; she wasn't asking for anything, she wasn't seeking a mirage. What she had gone through was everything *but* a mirage, it was the truth. She felt lucky because for a short while, her fairy tale had become a reality and her prince had finally come out of the pages of her fairy tale and was beside her; a simple, normal man with a big heart, a rich internal world and a strong character that made him stand out in the crowd. And she, who at the start, saw him as an opportunity to get away from blackmail, ended up giving her soul to him. She showed him who she was, she opened up her heart to him, and whatever she received from him, she gave back double.

When the fairy tale ended (and unfortunately the ending wasn't a happy one, and thus it wasn't at all targeted at children), Paulina fell into hibernation. The part of her ego that was hungry for food had been satisfied but at the same time she had ceased to exist. She hid her fairy tale somewhere deep inside and only visited it from time to time. She only pulled it out to the surface once a year, on the 17th of September, when she went to the Monastery of the Fools and lit a candle; one for her family and one for him.

Now she lived in London where she worked for the same advertising company as before. She had her children with her. Demetris, her husband, had sadly passed away three years beforehand in a terrible car accident. Although in a critical condition, she managed to speak to him at the hospital before he passed away. He was in a coma but she was sure that he had heard her.

She apologised for the times she hurt him and promised him that she would do whatever he wished for the children and herself. Demetris died in hospital two days later and he never found out about Paulina's wrong doing.

He loved her and they were good friends especially the last couple of years when their differences subsided. He was older than Paulina by thirteen years and he was never under the illusion that she had married him out of love. But they had good times together, they had two wonderful children and it was a shame that he left so unjustly and soon. Their children cried, so did Paulina. In the evenings, and on her own. In her daily routine she had to be strong and make decisions for her family. This is how a little while after her husband's death she decided to grasp the opportunity that was offered to her. To go to London.

She had studied there and had a British passport. Her mother had ignored everyone around her when she was seven months pregnant, and left on vacation to England with her husband. There, they were admiring the Elgin Marbles at the British Museum when suddenly she went into labour. Fortunately, they had enough relatives and friends there that helped them out. Two days after her mother was taken to hospital as an emergency, Paulina was born.

Paulina was named after the sweetest nurse that had stood by her mother as a sister would have and since then, the two women became close and built a friendship that would last for a lifetime. In the end, you can only classify people in two vast categories, because if you try anything else you are doomed. You can categorise them into good and bad; those who are made of a good paste and those who aren't. And Pauline, the nurse, was anything but the latter.

It was to be a big lesson learnt by her parents because they didn't particularly like English people yet they experienced what they did in England. Why would anyone want to discuss about the differences between Cypriots and foreigners, blacks and whites, about Christians and Muslims. The best discrimination is done when referring to the good and the bad people.

Paulina kept in close contact with Pauline, as did her mother. Now that she was living in England they became even closer.

Sometimes, on Sundays, she would go and visit Pauline in her house. She lived in Muswell Hill where she owned a small house opposite the park, with her partner Kieran. They weren't married; neither of them wanted to have children and thus there was no reason to. Nonetheless, they were together and in love for years. She was a nurse; he was a doctor, a heart surgeon with a good name and great expertise. He was a simple man, clever and very low key; a man who on a daily basis held the lives of many in his hands. Lives of people who came from all corners of the world to be operated upon in England since the standard of healthcare was enviable there.

Kieran, like a ferryman of a lake, gave life and death; *he* decided who would go to the underworld and who wouldn't. He was a simple, balanced guy that loved Pauline, Paulina and her children. And whenever they went to their house to have dinner, he cooked them superb roast lamb combined with spaghetti, Pauline's specialty, and an excellent panna cotta prepared by Paulina was what made their fiesta.

The children played in the garden or walked with the adults in the park, where they were having a little conversation and fresh air. The park was like a lung in a town that was drowning in fumes and pollution. Due to the sunshine, the parks were filled with people who lay in the grass, read books, played ball and cricket. Others took off their shirts and sunbathed. The sun was necessary in these cold and dark countries. People needed to warm not only their bodies but their mood, they needed to smile.

In a park in England you can definitely pinpoint the season just by looking around you. In spring everything is blooming, flowers are everywhere, thousands of colours and smells surround you. Visitors multiply; they go on boat rides on the lakes that decorate the parks of the English capital. In the summer you can find people walking down the streets and laying on the grass, always under the sun. Around noon they leave their workplace and move around like ants towards the parks, where hundreds of people sit on benches or on the ground and read newspapers or eat their sandwiches.

If you go to the park in autumn you will see trees almost naked, leaves laid out like a blanket on the floor and the trees provide oxygen to the residents of the capital. Quite a few Londoners wear their light jackets and are accompanied by their dogs, with which they run and exercise – which completes the image.

In winter, with the unbearable cold, the ducks, like magic, disappear. Some lakes freeze, while everything else around you is soaking wet.

Pedestrians are few; they walk at a fast pace, with overcoats and umbrellas. From time to time, you pinpoint winter tourists in their raincoats, mainly the Japanese who look left and right in awe, wearing their photo cameras around their necks.

These are the parks of London, the green oases in the big city, the parks that relax people, the parks that had always calmed Paulina down too. They openheartedly offered her their embrace during her endless walks through labyrinths of trees, romantic alleys, lakes and small hills. She would take in the views within the trees and flowers and she would get lost in thought. She would think of her children, her future and her husband who had died. At times, she would think of Dionysis and wished that God looked after him wherever he was.

Paulina looked up to Kieran and his relationship with Pauline. They treated each other with politeness, respect and love. She admired him because he was a doctor and from a young age she admired doctors for the work they did. Doctors and pilots; because so many lives depended on these two professions. Kieran, besides the fact that he was a great surgeon, was also a good man and he had treated her as a daughter from the very beginning. He helped her and he and Pauline became her family in England. Paulina had always kept in contact with Pauline but now that she had moved to England their friendship had grown even stronger.

Paulina had that good in her. She believed in the past, in memories, in people who had once played an important role in her life. She was a person dedicated to her friends and willing to respond to their needs, more substantially, in harder times than in easy ones. She avoided weddings and social obligations, but on the contrary went to funerals as she felt that people's feelings were more genuine on these occasions. There was honesty, support towards the other's pain and no hypocritical smiles.

Of course, she was influenced by the life in Cyprus where she grew up and where marriage was considered as the biggest commercial act someone could indulge in. Thousands of guests lined up in a queue for casual wishes. People went through the discomfort and all that work just for a good profit. These things now seemed so small and far away from her.

Small because of all the years that had gone by since her own wedding as well as the situations she had gone through which made her see life from a different angle, to reflect and judge. From afar, now that she had a foreign country as her shield and distance as her ally, she had – on the whole – said goodbye to these domestic obligations and not only these. Friends of friends, baptisms, engagements, marriages, dinners, an endless list of social conventions that reproduced habits and mentalities that go back years before and which, on many occasions, oblige you to casually rather than essentially participate in.

Of course there are people who really do like these ceremonies, who consider them as rituals, tradition or something that gives meaning to life. Paulina respected this; what she didn't respect were all the people who said 'what can we do about it, that's how things are' or people who called upon big philosophies and judged others and when their time came they would do exactly the same thing, if not worse.

She got angry with herself. Why was she thinking about all of this now? And anyhow, who was *she* to judge others? But that was exactly what was hurting her, the fact that she had gone through this, a woman who in her twenties was pressured to play a role that didn't represent her and she didn't react, she went along with the flow...anyone's flow. A time came when she realised this but it was too late. She recalled Father Ieroclis's words when finally she decided to go and confess as she felt that the time was right.

"Marriage, my child, is not obligatory and the people who consider it an obligation are wrong. It's a blessing, and people have to understand this and respect it before they proceed to action. Do you know," he said, "that it's only the woman who gets married?"

She looked at him in query. He referred to the Greek word for marriage, which when looked at literally means to get into a situation under a man. The Greek form is υπαντρεύομαι. Before she could react he continued talking.

"And *'under'* refers to obedience, respect and love. Not possessiveness. Husband and wife are equal because, simultaneously, the man has as many obligations towards his wife; to love her and respect her and to protect her."

How many of these things had Demetris honoured? Enough, much more than other people she had known, but Paulina herself, being a correct person, felt unworthily, unworthy of forgiveness.

"A husband, my child, doesn't get married, he gets a bride. A couple is therefore two people, a husband and wife, who walk together, pull the same weight. It's two trees, which by themselves lean towards each other in the wind and tie their branches together in order to endure more. In the beginning these branches get pruned in order to attain strength and, it goes without saying, that there is a lot of pain due to the new situation. Then love and unity gives them strength and they move on as one."

"Beautifully said," Paulina had thought, idealistic and correct. "There must be love that is a product of Eros though. When you begin on the wrong foot is when you need to find mutual ground." She didn't agree with everything that the priest had said, at times she would leave angry, others confused; she carried on going to see him though and slowly-slowly the bridges came down, she started to calm down, her heart lightened and she confessed to everything.

That was Paulina, a polite and patient person; someone who, when she believed in something, gave it all. She gave faith in whomever she loved, family, friends, Dionysis…

When she first arrived in London she had a hard time. Difficulties and paths less travelled are for the brave ones to walk upon and those who stand out in a crowd.

She lived in a beautiful small flat that the company had found for her in East Finchley and she enrolled her kids in school. She planned things through well there. Her daughter, Sophia was thirteen years old, and if she took on this job transfer for five years, her daughter would be ready to enter university when Paulina would return to Cyprus. Her son, Anastasis would return to Cyprus with her to complete his final two years of schooling and then he would go to the army before he would himself return to England to carry out further studies.

At work things were going well and she went up the ladder quite soon; she earned different promotions. She worked hard; nothing is coincidental in life, especially in these countries. The more of yourself you put in life, the more you will be rewarded. And Paulina invested a lot in her work and she progressed.

She wasn't a career woman; neither did she seek that. What she did though, she did well and she loved it. And when you are focused on what you do, you like it and you work hard and methodically you have nothing else to do but to succeed. Recently, she had got a new assignment and this is probably one of the reasons she was still in London.

They had called her from her office one morning a few weekends back and told her that they urgently needed her for a great job. A big publishing house in London was to take on the rights of a book written by a Cypriot writer who lived in Athens. This book was a huge success in Greece and there was a good possibility that it would do well abroad too. The publishing house approached her company to take on the promotion of the book.

A team would be put together that would prepare an action plan and Paulina was to be part of that team because, besides her qualifications, she also spoke the mother tongue of the writer.

She had heard about the writer but not much. She wasn't a book person herself, although she did read from time to time if something noteworthy fell in her hands. But this Yiannis Aidonidis had escaped her. She was happy he was a compatriot. 'Good on him,' she thought, 'the man surpassed his limits; he published a book in the Greek field and now he was trying for England and Ireland.'

She took some notes, wrote a questionnaire with interesting questions and decided, on the following Monday morning, to call Katy, a colleague and friend in Cyprus, to gather as much information as she could and ask her to send her a copy of the book as soon as possible so that she could read it for herself. They had put her in charge of this in any case. "One of us has to read the book in order to know what we are talking about," and of course Paulina was the ideal person for this.

On Monday morning she went to the office with a feeling that she herself couldn't define. Anticipation, and an undeterminable fear. Nostalgia for something indescribable. An internal need just like the kids' game 'hot or cold'. When you get very close to something someone else has hidden from you, they warn you that you are getting very, very hot (close) to it and you are taken over by distress.

She soon got into her routine; she had some work to hand in and she liked to keep her promises.

Around eleven she knew that in Cyprus, being two hours ahead, it was around the time when working people would have their lunch break. In a hurry she picked up her phone and called Katy. Thankfully, on the third ring her friend answered the call.

"Hi Katy, it's Paulina."

"Hi Paulina, how are you, it's been ages since we've spoken to each other, about two months or so?"

"Yes, approximately. You know I think about you often but we are all on a train that travels at a frantic pace and no one stops to have a look at themselves, even for a little while."

"Come on," said her friend's joyful voice, "you don't need to justify yourself. You and I know what connects us together, no need to say more. As far as our life is concerned, I think you're right; we're all 'on a plug'. The decease of cities, that's how all these phenomena are referred to. An endless immoral circle of tiredness, bad sleep, stress, wars about big money in order to achieve what? Just to pay off the debts that our megalomania for material and consumer goods has created, and that is the paradox, we have no time to enjoy it. But come on, tell me what you're up to, when will we have you back here with us?"

Paulina was happy to hear her friend's warm-hearted tone of voice.

"I was thinking of leaving at the end of July, to take some time off, but now a new job has popped up, which I have to confess is also the reason why I am calling you. So, I don't see myself coming before the middle of September, and only for a couple of days."

"And what's this – so important job – that keeps you away, and what does it have to do with us?"

Paulina explained to her friend the logistics of things and told her exactly what she wanted.

Katy sounded enthused.

"I have the book, I've read it. I'll go and buy it for you tomorrow and send it to you by courier. You'll have it by Thursday morning the latest. Paulina, you've never read anything like it. I don't know what words to use to describe it. True, moving, a human story. Well done. And I'm sure that this story has something to do with a personal experience of his, I may even say that it has to do with his story."

Paulina started to feel her curiosity growing. "We have said so much and you haven't even told me the title of the book."

"'*Witnessed by God and the moon,*' that's the title."

Paulina felt a slight pinch in her heart and butterflies in her stomach. She couldn't explain her disturbance. She asked her friend about the content of the book, but she denied telling her anything.

"Be patient, you'll have it in a couple of days. Whatever I tell you it won't do it any justice. It's a good opportunity to read something from one of your compatriots."

They continued talking, the conversation diverted to their children, they talked about other common interests and said goodbye.

Paulina was sceptical. In the beginning she felt that this whole story, this new job had messed up her plans. Now she was impatient and she wanted to know as much as she could about the writer Yiannis Aidonidis and of course, to read his book.

The Big Decision

Dionysis squeezed his heart and decided to leave Cyprus. He wanted to escape from a small place where people, with good or bad intentions, talk about you and pay attention to gossip. He had reacted quickly.

He had ended a marriage with a divorce with consequences against him, a marriage that was hanging by a string and held back his good intentions for the most part. He picked himself up and decided to take a road less travelled; he stopped pretending and took on the consequences. His marriage was condemned. It's never one person's fault. Often, people are like mirrors – they reflect what you show them and vice versa.

He was certain that the deeply rooted virtues that he had given to his children would not be lost. The relationship he had with them from the day they were born was ideal. Even when tired, drowned to his neck in his wife's family businesses, their relationship was strong.

He was brought up and taught about life in a hard way. Dionysis had lost his mother at a very young age and never felt the love and support that a mother can offer.

Once, he had read a small verse you sometimes come across in the back of diaries that had a huge impact on him: "God didn't have enough time to spread love everywhere and that's why he created mother". He grew up with his father, who was a father, the mother and the brother that Dionysis never had all at once. They say that when you grow up without brothers or sisters you become egoistic, but Dionysis was an exception to the rule.

He was always smiling, he thrived on giving. His orphaning from mother had given him a harshness that sometimes spooked people when they heard the grim thoughts that crossed his mind. Dionysis was a born leader and this seldom allowed him to remain silent or anonymous. This anonymity, which he suddenly sought out, was the second reason why he had decided to leave Cyprus.

The motherly love that he never got enough of, the virtues that his father gave him, all these 'ghosts', fairy tales and rich worlds that he used to make up as a child, he tried, and to a great extent, managed to pass on to his boys, Nicholas and Evgenios. Often, he told them imaginary stories that he himself created about good and bad, about princes and different kinds of Cinderellas.

He taught them how to respect, how to give, how to think of their fellow human beings and how to be a good judge. That's why, before he left, he knew that the hurt imposed on him by his divorce, the unpleasant consequences that would take place in his relationship with his sons and ex-wife would slowly subside. At some point, things would get better...easier.

He wanted to live in Thessaloniki, somewhere where he knew nobody, start from the beginning – all over again. A friend of his, Costas, had stood by him through these difficult times, which were full of obstacles and difficult decisions.

He lent him a large sum of money with which Dionysis would pay off all his debts and have some left over so he could get back on his feet for a couple of months. He also left some money in his personal account in the bank with a direct debit to pay his children's maintenance on a monthly basis.

Costas was also the one who took him to the airport. Before he left, Dionysis had asked him for a last favour; to pass by the Monastery of the Fools. They got there on a Friday afternoon in August. He wanted to say goodbye to his friend, Father Ieroclis.

Costas was surprised by his friend's wish because he knew he wasn't close to the church.

"Costas, every one of us, coincidently or not, finds a place – somewhere to sit down and reflect – which inspires them, impresses them and fills them with devoutness. For me, this place is this monastery in the middle of nowhere. I came here for the first time many years ago and since then it has been *my* place. Then I met the priest, and we became friends. Imagine how excited I was when I found out he was one of my father's classmates when they were young. I brought them back in contact. I go and find him and we discuss anything. It has always helped me; God, the nuns and the fools. Father Ieroclis always helped me find solutions to my problems."

Costas realised the importance of his friend's words and respected it. This is also perhaps why he asked to find out more about the monastery.

"I'll make it hard on you," said Dionysis, "I'll let you find out the history of the monastery on your own. There is no one who can tell it better than Sister Ilaria."

"She's the one who told you the story?"

"Yes, the first time I came to the monastery I found her in the church; we started talking, she offered me sweets, they make delicious lemon sweets there, then she told me the story. Since then this place became my place."

During their conversation of their imminent destination they arrived at the monastery. They prayed, drank water and sat on a bench in the shade until the priest appeared. Dionysis kissed the priest's hand and then they hugged.

The old priest, with his unforeseen young way of thinking, talked to them a little, he read a wish to them inside the little church and suddenly he looked at Dionysis very seriously.

"So you're finally leaving my son?"

"Yes father, I'm leaving and I'll be coming and going for the children. I'll be taking them to Thessaloniki once a year with me too, if all goes well. I'm going to try and have everything sorted out by next Easter."

"Dionysis, my child, we've discussed enough. The only thing I have left to do is to give you my blessing, may God be with you. I will give you something else as well, a letter for the Monk Vonifatio, who you will find on Mount Athos, his hermitage. I want you to give it to him as soon as you can. I'll speak to him by phone and tell him to expect you."

Costas had been listening all this time and slowly realised the bond that connected these two men, the two completely different worlds that they had managed to combine through the holy bond of friendship.

Some time had elapsed; they had to go and they knew it. Dionysis said goodbye to the father and his eyes watered but he stood strong.

"Cry my son, cry as much as you want, you mustn't be ashamed. Crying is a sign of power and not weakness as many would like to think. Crying helps us with our own humiliation and self-criticism. Crying is a source of life…"

Truly, Dionysis cried in the car, he was overwhelmed with sorrow; the greatness of his departure from his children and everything that had happened in the past couple of days had all come up to the surface.

The scenarios that had developed two hours earlier in his birth home, where his children had come to say goodbye, flashed in front of his eyes like a big nightmare that dawned on him.

His youngest son played the tough guy; he still hadn't forgiven his parents for separating, and his logic told him that such things weren't allowed. The eldest son seemed to be in a better state; he had managed to internalise a couple of feelings perhaps, but who knows. 'Did this really happen?' Dionysis said over and over again in his mind.

He had hugged both of them in his arms and had barely managed to give them any advice. He told them to behave and listen to their mother, to be friends and love each other, and that whatever they needed they should tell their grandfather and call him all together.

Then he hugged his father and their good neighbour Ms Kallistheni and moved along towards the car. Only when Costas started the car and started moving did the youngest son Evgenios start running behind them in an outburst of tears until the car stopped. At the car he hugged his father with as much strength as he had and let go of what he couldn't express to other adults, his sorrow. On the spot, it was like he remembered that he had the right to be angry and hurt, then he ran towards the house and went inside.

Dionysis returned to the car and, like a robot, he felt as though his blood wasn't flowing through his veins. He remained completely still from the hurt. He couldn't define if his heart had stopped beating; nevertheless, it was hurting him tremendously.

Revealed and redeemed from the weight that he had had on his chest for such a long time now, he lit a cigarette and turned to his friend.

"Costas, I will never forget what you've done for me. I will pay you back soon. After the first six months I'll start paying you off on a monthly basis as we agreed. I need some time to get back on my feet first though."

Costas nodded and smiled.

"Dionysis, I know you're a man who keeps his word, so stop talking about it; you judge and act as you think is right. I trust you, and I know you'll get through this."

"Costas, you stood by me like the brother that I never had. A friend is sometimes more precious than family because you get to choose them. There is something else I have to tell you and I want you to keep it to yourself. There is a story that no one knows about. I have kept it to myself for various reasons but mostly out of respect for the other person involved. I have a woman kept safely inside of me like an amulet in my heart. She was also the reason why I divorced, without her forcing me to do so though. Her presence helped my marriage more than anything else; she made me calm, and made me see things differently.

"Our love was platonic and it grew. When things got difficult and everything was in danger of being revealed, I chose to protect her name and marriage. As for me, I decided to get a divorce because I had to face the truth, both in regards to my life *and* my marriage to Cleo.

"Years ago, Cleo and I 'closed the door' on each other and since I committed many other sins, most of them being casual relationships.

"I was however, always secure, in a routine with my children. In a world that we all build around us. Today, when I look around me I wonder if this world is real for most people. Some other time, I might tell you more about this woman, but now that you have been to the monastery, I want to ask you for a favour. I want you to come to the monastery every year on the 17th of September and light two candles, one for me and one for her. That's the day I met her and it means a lot to me."

Costas's eyes filled from emotion. He knew his friend was sensitive and more importantly, that he cared about others. He had confirmed this now. That's why he promised him, with all his heart.

The Vow

Even the longest paths begin with one step, the first step. Dionysis arrived in Thessaloniki and started organising himself straight away. The first days were difficult, not only because it was a foreign place to him, but also because of his financial situation and his immediate need to find a job. Along with this came his mental situation and the feeling of not wanting to get out of bed in the morning. Losing your orientation, your goals, being hurt, not wanting to see anyone and only wanting to roll over on the other side and fall asleep again. You don't want dawn to come, but the first light comes through anyway, at some point; the hours of the clock unstoppably tick by and the day invites you to take on your responsibilities. It calls upon you to live. And Dionysis started to live again, slowly – slowly.

For now, he found a small, quiet two-bedroom flat on the third floor of a small apartment block, close to the centre of the town. He needed the second bedroom for when the children would come to visit. During the first couple of days he made sure he got to know all the construction companies and architectural offices in Thessaloniki and he started filling in applications. He sent his CV here and there and then, while he was waiting for a response, he started fixing his flat.

He bought some furniture, a small TV and a radio with a CD player and other electrical appliances. Then he painted the flat with care. Dionysis was a perfectionist. When it came to doing something, he liked to do it well.

Life had taught him that action was better than no action, even if you made mistakes. Actions, even if not always done successfully, were better than inactivity and criticism. He invested in his flat, put in a phone line and while waiting for the phone line to be connected he bought himself a cell phone in order to be able to be contacted by the various companies he had applied to. Indeed, he received a lot of calls.

His problem was another. When companies found out who he was and what his experience was, they were sceptical about offering him the job because he was overqualified for what they were looking for.

Until Diomidis Aristidou came along.

"I know you," he said to him bluntly. "I know your father-in-law well, or should I say your ex father-in-law; I must admit, he always had good things to say about you. Regardless of what happened between you and his daughter, I will hire you and I want you to prove to me that you're worthy. I may have a problem with your father-in-law because of this but he is a good man and I would like to believe that he wouldn't want the life of the father of his grandchildren to be ruined due to revenge. I have enough projects under development and I need help. You will come on board, in the second team of engineers, and we'll see. There are about fifteen of you and there are four engineers in the first team, which you report to."

Dionysis didn't get into details, he accepted the offer straight away and thanked the man while revealing to him that he was a man with dignity who will keep his distance and will earn his last penny with his own sweat. There was one last thing he needed to do before though; he thought about it for a while and then made his decision.

He wanted to go to Mount Athos to fulfil the promise he had made to himself, but also to deliver the letter that Father Ieroclis had given to him before he left Cyprus. He thought that the best time to do this was during the National Anniversary on the 26th to the 28th of October, which was a Bank Holiday. It wouldn't have been right to ask for time off work. He could have, but he didn't want to cross the line, this was in any case his way of life and a philosophy in which he believed in. Every man has to set his boundaries on his own and set his limits alone. He himself has to know when to stop.

He doesn't need a policeman, a parent, a wife, a bank manager or a partner to set these limits for him. No one, no matter what they tell you, can stop you from doing *anything*.

One may have a desire to fulfil but hold it inside oneself, for the time being. Eventually, that desire and curiosity will grow up to a point where one cannot fight it anymore. If one grows up with strong virtues then one can set one's limits oneself, but how many people actually do? Every time people teased him about these strange ideals he lived by he would say that it's good to belong to the few and not the many and be different.

He booked his ticket for those dates and he would combine it with a weekend away. He felt good about himself. The weight on his shoulders had started to subside. It was the first time he enjoyed a routine and anonymity so much.

Sometimes, in life, some things and words carry some form of negativity because that's how we are socialised and conditioned to know about them. The word routine, for example, or the fact that living in big cities is lonely; but isn't it great just to be able to walk down the street where no one knows you, to be unshaven, to watch people and window-shop, to wear clothes you feel like wearing that don't match and not give a damn?

Another word that is misunderstood is Sunday. There is a Greek song composed by a Greek composer called Tsitsanis that goes "Clouded Sunday, you look like my heart". But Dionysis's Sundays were anything but cloudy. Sundays were the best day of the week for him. He usually worked on Saturday mornings and in the afternoon, exhausted, he would sleep for a while before going to a local tavern for dinner with a colleague or a large group of people.

But on Sundays…he talked to his children on the phone for a while and never had enough of listening to their achievements. His youngest son Evgenios was a little cold with him at first but gradually things got better.

His favourite time of day was in the afternoon when he went out for a walk, and sat in the small square next to his flat where he read a newspaper while drinking a coffee. That's when he put his thoughts in order, calculated his finances and made his plans, and on some occasions, had dreams. Secret dreams. Sometimes he would rent a car and go on an outing, sometimes by himself, other times with company. He liked driving and nature, daydreaming came easy to him.

He had always been a dreamer, he always thought about interesting things about his work and his life. He could create something from nothing. You could lock him in a room for hours and he would find something to keep himself busy. He created, he thought, he wrote, he took notes, and had done so ever since he was a child.

He didn't have a mother close to him and he had learnt to survive on his own. Once, at school, he was teased because he talked about something he believed they would learn in school during the next couple of years. Everyone teased him except his teacher who listened to him and gave him advice he never forgot. "Let them laugh, you stick to your guns, you're not funny or crazy, it's just that your ideas are not made for the masses yet. Remember your thoughts, though, and take courage by thinking that humanity has made progress because of people like you. People with a vision and insight, fools, who believed in things not because everyone else did or because they were doing the 'right' thing. Not even because they were intellects, conservative, super beings, or even because they were 'part of the establishment'." These were the words that stuck in his mind and soul.

Every Sunday night he also tried to call his father. Over the years, their relationship had strengthened. His father would tell him news from Cyprus, about Limassol specifically; Dionysis updated him on his news and time passed. The 26th of October came. He had to fulfil his vow and go to Mount Athos, and he did...

Sitting on a boat, which was taking him to the magical world of the monastic state of Athos, Dionysis smoked a cigarette and daydreamed. There were about fifteen other people with him but he didn't try to converse with anyone. He didn't want to. He wanted this time exclusively to himself. He felt that a lot recently. Everyone goes through different stages. Sometimes he wanted to be with people, others alone. Sometimes he listened, sometimes he spoke.

Dionysis learned to listen to people from a young age. He listened to the voices of people and fairies, as well as the voice of his mother; his mother wasn't there with him, she had died but she advised him from another world, the world of souls. He spoke to her in the evenings when his father and their neighbour Ms Kallistheni, a spinster who also used to babysit him sometimes, said goodnight to him.

Ms Kallistheni, alone and unlucky, was once engaged to someone who took all her money and then disappeared. She slowly accepted her fate and remained single. She was older than his father and when his mother died she started coming to their house; she cooked and looked after Dionysis. She may also have been satisfying some of Mr Nicolas's as well as her own needs perhaps.

In the end, we accommodate ourselves and that's not such a bad thing. Many times, straightforward arrangements, those that apply no pressure or obligation, bring out good results. No oppression, no jealousy. But you never know. What are straight forward arrangements? As many explanations as you can try to give to someone, you cannot exclude the human factor or some weaknesses. Although two people can be straightforward about what they share together, the relationship at times can still be balancing on a tightrope. If animals, which are wild beasts, can get jealous, then why can't humans too; with all their varying feelings and logic?

Whatever the case, what Dionysis realised about his father's relationship with this older lady Ms Kallistheni, was that they seemed straightforward with each other. His father treated her well, she loved Dionysis and she never crossed the line; she never showed that she had any vested rights.

And that's how Dionysis grew up, with fairies whispering stories and nice words in his ears, with his mum advising him from the ideal world and his father playing different roles and enduring these. His father had the strength to raise his child well, not with too much pressure and not being too soft either. He watched his son grow from a distance and only interfered when he felt he needed to. On many occasions he let his son make mistakes, he didn't stick out for him for minor issues, he cultivated his son's sense of responsibility from a young age.

Dionysis, however, found out where his father got his strength from. One day, he went to his mother's grave as he usually did, to sit 'with her', talk to her, take care of her grave. When he approached the grave he noticed that someone was already there, his father, who was stroking the stunning marble slab of the grave and cried. Dionysis hid and listened to his father speaking to his mother, telling her sweet words. He remained in hiding until his father left.

He never told his father he had seen him, so as not to make him feel uncomfortable, but he felt lucky because he realised he had special parents. He felt special himself too and realised that other people also spoke with their deceased loved ones, their fairies. It was true, nowadays and at times, Dionysis missed the cemetery and his mother's grave.

He used to go there often and as he grew up he got used to going there to think, make decisions, beneath the old, tall Cypress trees. The cemetery was just like another town, with horizontal and vertical roads, small houses; the graves of the dead. Here, there weren't any rich and poor districts − luxury and misery coexisted. An old magnificent tomb, with a slab of black marble, just like a mausoleum, where a whole family slept, and next to them another one with a wooden cross, which was looked after with a lot of care, no weeds, well-watered flowers and a lit candle.

Dionysis heard voices, imaginary and real voices. The more he heard them, the more he learnt. He was like a sponge that greedily sucked in water and was only satisfied with wisdom and knowledge. He listened to his father, his teacher, elderly people, his competitors and co-workers and then he made decisions accordingly. This is how he managed to do things well; he had his own way of doing things and, besides becoming a good engineer, he became a first-class business man.

What then went wrong with his marriage, how did he reach this point? He lit a second cigarette and looked around him. They say that the sea relaxes you, that it has a magical attribute to it; its fragrance and the air that surrounds it, its sound that clears the mind. If the sea can relax you, imagine what the seas that gush at the foot of Mount Athos can do to you. There, the noises and the deep green colour of the water create holiness and a devout atmosphere that eventually enriches the soul of any visitor. It was obvious to him now; he felt his blood flowing in his veins, he felt overwhelmed by a tremendous elation and euphoria that passed through his body as he looked, heard and felt everything around him. 'Everything will be fine,' he said to himself while reaching for his pocket to make sure that he had the letter that he was to deliver to Father Vonifatios.

The respected father lived alone and led a self-disciplined life in a hermitage close to the monastery. Dionysis had decided to go and find him on the spot. He didn't want to be a tourist, he didn't have time for that anyhow, and besides Mount Athos wasn't for tourism. He wanted to go to the monastery, relax, see the venerable father, think and perhaps pray. Of course he didn't know to what level of thought, ecstasy, awe or peacefulness he would reach, nevertheless...

No one can understand what Mount Athos represents unless they visit it, as like all things unknown to us for that matter. If you tried to explain academically what the word 'hunger' meant it would be very different than having to understand it by feeling hungry, not because of lacking time to eat but because of not having food to eat. The meaning of words changes according to the way in which you experience them.

Once again Dionysis got lost in his own world. The difficult phases in his life seemed to have subsided. In Thessaloniki he was making his new home and had plunged into his work. It was going well but he missed his children terribly. Some say that some people have a bigger weakness for their sons and others for their daughters and they insist to differentiate between the two. This is unjust. How can a parent love one child more than another? This cannot be, nor can love be shared. If you have two children, is it possible to split your love in two and if you had five children, to split it in five? You cannot divide love, you can only multiply it and it is always equal; you can always give as much as you want, if you look deep inside, regardless of how many children you may have.

This weakness though, a word everyone uses and which Dionysis never admitted to because it made him feel guilty, he possessed for his youngest son. And he knew why. His youngest son's actions reminded him of his own when he was a child. His facial expressions, his reactions, his internal world, reminded him vividly of his own. He recalled the times when he went to high school and he started being interested in girls. The first glances, the first messages. His classmates always preferred older boys who were more mature in body and mind. He was also mature, seeing as he had grown up suddenly when his mother died but girls didn't pay much attention to him. As time went by his experiences multiplied, he created a strong personality and he had a strong opinion. It was strange, but what else do people have than strangeness? Many girls besieged him during his last year of school and he 'loved' a girl from the class next to his who didn't seem to have any interest. She probably didn't know about Dionysis's interest because he never dared to confide it to her. Up until one evening, when they met at a party where they were introduced and eventually talked and danced.

He accompanied her home on his bicycle that night and once home she thanked him and told him that she had had a lovely evening but that they couldn't meet again because she had a boyfriend that she loved but they had had a fight that night and that was why she was alone. She leaned forward and kissed him on the cheek and left. Sensitive as he was Dionysis held on to that kiss for years to come, a keepsake of a young, innocent touch.

It's strange how many times you hear that so and so likes a girl and that she likes someone else and that someone else is going out with a friend of hers but you know that deep inside (the friend) loves another person and so on, an endless chain. It seems like no one ever finds his or her match, but things aren't like that. People just compromise. They stop searching, and each of them settles in one way or another.

Maybe we should throw all the men in a box and all the women in another and have them reshuffled all over again, by chance. Perhaps only then will the world be at rest, maybe the downhill will stop and the smiles, love and happiness will start all over again.

Even when Dionysis eventually had a girlfriend he would put himself down and when he saw another girl that he had liked in the past, he once again didn't know what to do about it. He was thirsty for experiences and on many occasions he would double date. He always had the girl who gave him the gentle kiss on the cheek in his mind, the ideal woman, and from then on it seemed like many women, up to a certain point, paid the price for the walls that he had built around himself. He finished with the army, he went to study and he was doing well, but he always kept something to himself. The sweet girl in question as well as other plans that he had made for himself had prevented any woman from even trying to get closer to him.

As he sat there he reminisced all of this and smiled with nostalgia, or even with some form of shame. He wasn't a jerk, nor did he sell love, and he didn't lie. He was tender, but no woman stayed for long. Either he seized the relationship or they kicked him away, or they separated as friends.

All until he met Cleo who managed to win him over. It may have also been the right time. You see, sometimes, many things have to fit together in order for something to happen. The universe has to converse, as Coelho says. The point is for the universe not to converse against you…

'Love,' he thought, 'did I really love the young girl with the sweet face that kissed me on the cheek or was it a frivolity, an enthusiasm?' No, no, that was unfair; you can't sit around for nearly forty years and suddenly, sitting on a boat, start thinking about enthusiasm with certainty. At the time, in his teenage years and dreams, feeling and acting the way he did he must have loved her. A man becomes tougher with the years but he doesn't change; he would probably, if it happened to him again, fall in love with her all over again.

He was suddenly enlightened. The girl of his dreams had a sweet smile, dark brown eyes, short black hair, and white skin. He closed his eyes and tried to picture her. He tried to go back in time and draw her in his mind and to his surprise he drew Paulina. As much as he tried to separate them, two visions became one.

He tried to alternate the pattern in his mind and thought about Cleo. And in order to anticipate himself, before he said anything silly about frivolity, wrong doings and enthusiasm, he opened his eyes instantly.

The boat was floating in the blue waters, everyone on the boat was minding their own business, no one paid much attention to Dionysis and he lost himself in thoughts once again. How could his two boys be a mistake? If we all had this fear we should lock ourselves into a house and do nothing all day and all night long, then, certainly, we would make no mistakes. Is there a bigger mistake than this though? Not to do anything because of fear, to sit on one side and watch the cardiograph of time, thus your life, go by and implore you to love while you watch a straight line being created on a monitor, then being printed on a piece of paper and in the end signing your own death sentence?

If suicide is a sin, it's a weakness; is there a bigger sin than complete resignation? To live for eighty years but already be dead by the time you are thirty?

Cleo had long blonde hair, dark skin and greyish green provocative eyes; a big bust as he liked. She knew how to blend in with people; she always dressed well, almost too well. And they hit it off; one could say that they loved each other. In any case, no one obliged them to stay together, no one pressured them. But why was he tormenting himself with all this now, their relationship didn't work out; it wasn't the first time, or the last...

He thought about Paulina again. Yes, Paulina represented a princess to him, the princess of his dreams. A wicked witch had put a curse on her and when she grew older she would fall into an endless sleep and would only awake if someone loved her for what she was and if he loved her more than himself.

Was Paulina real or just a wish that had never come true, something that had drifted away at some point because of a rejection and a kiss on the cheek from another Paulina, a Paulina that was thirteen years old? From time to time Dionysis lost track of things because after so many years he still wasn't sure whether he was in love and with whom.

He wasn't even sure what love was, how Eros leads to love and what true love was. He had the impression that the deprivation of certain people in his life, the fact that he was married and so was Paulina was what turned the flame into fire, which in turn made both their hearts beat like crazy but also nearly burnt both of them. Or maybe it was due to the fact that their meetings were so limited with time that they both brought out the best of themselves, they put their best clothes on and treated each other with so much tenderness, so much respect, kindness and discretion.

On the other hand, he thought that things weren't like this at all, that Paulina was, even now, even after the near scandal, what he had always looked for in life. The love, the kick-start, the warm embrace, the holding of the hand, the eyes, the tremor of the voice, the person you want to do the most simple things with. The person you will see at their worst times and still love, the person that when you smell their sweat after a long day at work you yearn for. A person that even when they annoy you, you will love them; a person that will endure you as you are. A person who when you leave on a trip will wish you to have a good time and will worry but not show it. A person who will, above all, treat you well and will be the last person to take you for granted. A person who when you make a foolish mistake or act like a pig will tell you and treat you so well that you will feel like a complete pig and you will swear never to hurt that person again.

What he dreamt of was what always happens during the last two minutes of a film, what always happens in fairy tales when a couple gets married and celebrates for three whole days and nights and lives happily ever after, that was Dionysis and Paulina.

Yes, he had taken her out of a mediocre life, he knew her more than she knew herself and slowly he let her get on to the bridges of his soul. He opened up the gates of his internal world and he helped her get to know his world and who he was. And the girl with the sweet smile took flesh and bone and cured an old wound. And he filled her life with flowers.

And then he thought about the fact that they were both unjust to their partners. They were unjust towards the bringing up of their children and their difficulties, their home, their daily routine, practical things, social obligations, routine, stress. Enthusiasm settles; eros, if existent, subsides. A love is born more out of need and then someone else comes along that upsets the stagnant waters and levels out everything, that's hypocrisy or a frivolity. 'It's just like a trial,' thought Dionysis.

The defendant claims that there is love and that it is eternal. Opposite him the public defendant that stands on behalf of society, claims that all and everything wears out, that all begins well and gradually things wear out. All of this is natural, this is the path, and you can't talk about love and Eros after a certain age or after you have spent a certain amount of time with a person. Erotic love gives its place to a love that is more like a fellowship, a habit.

In Virgin Mary's Orchard

Every attempt to describe Mount Athos; the monasteries, the monks and the feelings that are inflicted on visitors, don't justify reality. That's why I haven't tried to do so.

Some information may be enough to awaken the curiosity of the reader and prompt a visit to Mount Athos. A small state, one would call it, which majestically takes over the eastern of the three 'legs' of the Khalkidhiki peninsula, the one closer to Turkey.

The way is simple. A taxi from Thessaloniki to Ouranoupoli and from there, once you've got your '*dianomitirio*' (your accommodation details) that you have already booked by phone, and once you have presented your passport, you take the boat from a small harbour to Daphne. There, large jeeps await you and take visitors to the monasteries, while other smaller boats reach the monasteries by sea.

Dionysis, like other visitors, arrived at a time when visits were scarce (as he preferred). He left thousands of thoughts back on the boat and got out at Daphne to go to the small monastery he had chosen. He got into another boat with other visitors and mentioned who he was, where he wanted to go and sat patiently looking around him continuously, admiring the landscape, looking at things and people while trying to realise where he was.

He reached the monastery on Saturday just before noon and he was to leave on Monday noon. They put him in a room where six other people stayed although there were only four at the time including him. As far as the schedule of the monastery was concerned, it was similar to all monasteries with small alternations from one monastery to another and which, just for the benefit of the reader, I concisely mention.

Wake up call before daylight breaks for the matins and ceremony. Around seven in the morning there is a *Trapeza*; a meal that lasts for about half an hour which starts and ends for everyone at the same time. Between 7.30 and 12.30 various activities take place, for instance, agricultural work, hagiography etc. Then, there is a resting period before vespers at 4.30. At six in the evening, dinner follows and then the evening service, a small function that lasts for fifteen minutes where people come to worship the Holy Remains. After that, there is a study period, prayers and rest. Sleep until three in the morning where a new day begins once again.

These last hours are important because every monk goes back to their cell and communicates with God; by reading, writing, and a lot of praying. Each one tries to find God in himself, perfection, to combat their passions and sins and find holiness. As for the faithful pilgrims, Dionysis could not be an exception.

He reached the monastery a little before noon and went straight into following the programme. It was Saturday and he was to stay there until Monday. He was determined to take as many supplies, mostly spiritual, as he could before he left the holy place. He made himself comfortable in the room they gave him, besides he didn't bring many things and this didn't bother him at all. He ate one of two *Loukoumia(Greek delights)* and drank *Tsipouro(a strong alcoholic drink),* which they offered in the guest house, he rested a while and then went to vespers. He wanted to pray, listen to the service, think; He sat on a bench at the back of the small church where the service was taking place and once again drifted into a monologue of self-criticism.

'Here I am on Mount Athos, a remotely conceived destination that has become reality. So many years had to pass by and certain things had to happen to me in order to get here. Work was always in the way, obligations, family, this and that. They say that now that I have made the effort to come here I will come every year; let's see. I have reached my Mecca, my Ganges River, my Tibet, my Orthodox expiatory.

'I am thirty-nine years old, divorced, with a great deal of experiences, some good, some bad and I'm starting afresh. I start my second circle with a mediocre job, no money, with a small rented flat and without a car. Let's see where this one will take me.'

He suddenly felt very free. All what he had lost, with a big exception the contact, embrace and presence of his children, wasn't that important. There was nothing he couldn't fix. Yes, he surely felt free. He had escaped from a different prison, a prison of selfishness, favours, consideration, money, social obligation with no spiritual feedback and many 'musts'. He was hurt and naked but he could smell the fresh air, literally *and* metaphorically. The memory of his boys hit him again. Yes, this was his deepest wound, the biggest price to pay; he had to work on this.

Late in the afternoon, food was served; sparing but tasteful. He started feeling better; he started speaking to two fellow travellers and with one or two monks. He asked about the hermitage of the venerable father and he found out what he wanted.

A little while later, it got dark and since he was used to a different routine, he didn't want to go to sleep. In any case he had only come here for a couple of days; he was determined to go through these days with no sleep and take in as many things as he could.

The monks, after having finished their chores, started parting one by one. Dionysis stayed behind with his roommates whom he had now met since they were sharing the same room. The night was beautiful. They all agreed to sit on benches outside their cell with a view of the sea. They wouldn't go to bed late; they knew they had to wake up before dawn to go to the service. It was still very early though, dusk had set in, the moon was almost full, the atmosphere was sweet and night called upon them to attain a truce with themselves. This was the best place to do so.

They caught themselves chit-chatting and gradually these four strangers found common ground and started opening up to each other, confessing themselves. 'Strange,' thought Dionysis, 'it's the second time this has happened these past few months,' and his mind jumped to the stranger at the Monastery of the Fools who had stoically listened to his story and pain with no criticism.

This time round he preferred to be more of a listener than a speaker, but he participated in his own way. One of them, Andreas, the oldest one of the group, had lost his wife whom he deeply loved and had come to Mount Athos to find comfort. The other, Aristarchos, from Thessaloniki, had been indebted and seemed tormented. He was roughly Dionysis's age but seemed much older.

Dionysis summed him up and concluded that he was a good person. He listened to him carefully and gave him some brief advice. Being into business himself, he understood quickly where things may have gone wrong. They exchanged phone numbers and agreed to meet in Thessaloniki; besides, they lived in the same city. The other one slowly calmed down and one could define a small hope on his face, as it faintly appeared in the moonlight which was rising slowly in the open sky.

The last of the group was Mitros, around twenty-eight years old, who had just come out of prison. He had been in jail for four years for the usage and dealing of drugs. They say that the more sinful you are, the closer you will come to God. He had promised to himself that as soon as he came out of prison and specifically on his name day he would go to Mount Athos. He was neither from a divorced family, nor a poor one, nor did he have psychological problems. He came from a wealthy family and that's perhaps where the white death hits nowadays. It hits the doors of those who have a kind of financial draw. The myth about the least preferred social classes and the children of an inferior God is not valid anymore with regards to drugs. It knocks on all doors. And unfortunately once you get involved with it, you can rarely escape from it.

Dionysis recalled one of his favourite songs, 'Hotel California' by the Eagles, which metaphorically speaks about drugs and characteristically in one of its verses says 'you can check out any time you want, but you can never leave'. It's not always easy to get out of.

Mitros, however, escaped. He told them that he couldn't lie anymore and that in order to find money for his dose he started selling drugs and at one point they caught him. He went to jail and managed to survive by seeking help and, regardless of the unfavourable conditions, he got over his passion. When you manage to do this, you become very strong and wise and Mitros was standing in front of them today, with a sad look in his eyes and a tired smile, but you could identify a determination and thirst for life in his eyes, a good life, an honest one.

It seemed like an electric wave had passed through all of them because suddenly, they all drew energy from the young boy who had lived experiences that other people need two life times to experience. 'There are worse problems than mine,' thought Dionysis as he told them that he had just been through a divorce and had left Cyprus for a fresh start.

Sometimes chemistry works well between people. The timing, the place, the need. Or again, what I have mentioned before, everything happens for a reason, nothing is coincidental.

So many – thousands – of people come to Mount Athos, so many personalities. Mr Andreas, Aristarchos, Dionysis, and Mitros hit it off straight away, they heard each other, patted one another on the back and said 'courage'. It didn't matter whether they would meet again or not, what counted was the warmth that each of them individually and in their own way put in the heart and soul of others, regardless whether friendships were born or not, like the one that developed between Dionysis and Aristarchos.

As for Mr Andreas, he spoke to them about his wife and cried, he told them beautiful words, he revealed, insignificant perhaps, details about his wife's habits, their relationship, about her sickness and how calm and patient she was until the end. The rest of them didn't say much, they just surrendered to the greatness of human relationships that we all dream of and few find or can endure.

Often, you wonder how you can stand or sit in function for so many hours and endure it by not getting tired or impatient.

When he heard the soft knock on his bedroom door, Dionysis jumped up and woke up the others. It was cold and the water he splashed on his face was even colder, but the anticipation, curiosity perhaps, and the search, as well as the talk the evening before, had brought them all closer, warmed him up. The service was beautiful, their participation wasn't a chore and when you do something that isn't done by obligation time goes by quickly. In the candlelight, the voices of the monks' choir as well as the content of their words created an atmosphere of devoutness and holiness. Yes, the hours, the precious hours elapsed quickly but beautifully.

After the service came the meal, which everyone enjoyed. Sometimes it's all in the mind. I want that, or other, I want salt and oil and meat and anything else you can imagine. But here nothing like this occupied anyone. The food was tasty, and that was it. Then they were free to do what they wanted. A monk took a team with him and showed them around the monastery. He showed them the ins and outs, its history, the holy books, its pictures and the treasure of immeasurable historical and spiritual value, as well as various crafts; sewing, writing, hagiography, gardening and wine making.

Everyone felt good; they felt revived, for a while they forgot about their problems and gave themselves to what they had travelled here to do.

Eventually noon came around and they went to rest for a while but Dionysis who, in the meantime, had collected a lot of information about his goal, was anxious to meet the venerable Father Vonifatios.

It was afternoon, early…it started getting chilly and the sky attained a dark greyish-blue colour, while the sea below gave a deep-blue contrast. At the end of the horizon, where the sky meets some of the sunrays that had remained from the sunset, the last strokes of the painting of nature, made an artwork that created a beautiful feeling of harmony, nostalgia along with melancholy. In between all this, there was a tone of positivity and optimism for the days to come, which warmed their hearts.

Carrying all these feelings and with the envelope tucked in his left jacket pocket close to his heart, Dionysis felt it was time to meet with Father Vonifatios. He went out to the yard of the monastery and slowly started making his way down towards the hermitage. A sculpture, as they had described it to him, in a huge rock quite close to the sea, which, with a little imagination and human intervention had been transformed into a small room, a little home, the holy nest of the hermit.

As they had explained, he had to walk about half an hour along the length of a small path, which stood out slightly from the wild vegetation that enriched the area.

Dionysis started walking; in the beginning he walked slowly and gradually quickened his pace, his heart warming up to the chilly autumn afternoon. They had given him some supplies to take to the venerable father which he willingly took with him. They supplied him with food every two weeks and Dionysis had offered to take on this task. He was happy to be useful.

He put his saddlebag on his shoulder and set off. He took a torch with him in case he was late and would have to return in the dark. "You'll get there in half an hour," they had said, "and half an hour to get back. If you stay there for an hour and half you may be taken by dusk, at this time of year it goes dark around six…"

He walked and enjoyed the landscape around him. The anxiousness about meeting the venerable father created a feeling of euphoria in him, an optimistic mood that he hadn't felt in a long time. That's how it is, when you are hurt a lot you reach a nadir, physically and mentally conceived and whatever comes next can only be good. Recently good things *were* happening to him. As for the pain, due to the deprivation of his children, it had started getting more bearable, not because it receded but because he had started getting used to it and endured it better.

Plenty of oxygen, beautiful colours, a nice path, sounds of birds and animals, smells from the mountains and the sea all taken in and filtered by the holiness of the place. He started feeling in abeyance, far from his body, looking at himself moving along fast and steadily towards his destination.

He thought of the happenings, he thought of Father Ieroclis, the Monastery of the Fools. He hadn't felt like this in a long time and he moved on, and on.

'I must be close,' he said to himself. The path started going downhill suddenly, some big rocks started to appear, the ground was smoother and he smelled the sea closer as well. As he moved along he suddenly felt a strange tremor, an emotion, and he felt he wasn't alone anymore. He slowed down a little and looked left and right as he reduced his pace. His steps gradually brought him around the back of a huge rock that stood there as if it was guarding its unit all the while looking out at sea.

He tried to see how he could reach the front of the huge rock that probably hid the hermitage he was looking for. Far ahead, he could see an artery of the path that diverted behind bushes and if it turned slightly it would perhaps lead him to the front of the rock where the hermitage of the venerable father stood. Indeed, he followed his intuition and logic and gradually setting his right foot first for support and moving along slowly, he went down the small path which, after almost making a full circle, brought him in front of the cell. The cell itself consisted of a couple of basic spaces for the need of a human and outside there was a stool and a table.

"Father Vonifatios," called Dionysis.

No answer. He called again and at the same time, he moved in towards the entrance of the cell and started looking around. A candle was burning in front of two or three images of saints in a small curve within the wall. On the other side stood an old metal bed, a chair, another table, a gas-lamp, three or four books spread out on the table and many more laid on the bedside table next to the bed.

'Biographies of saints,' thought Dionysis as he prepared himself to call once again when a soft hand touched him gently on the shoulder.

"You made it my son," said the venerable father and smiled as Dionysis turned around. Getting over the initial fright, he returned the smile and ducked to kiss the venerable father's hand.

They both entered the cell and Dionysis put down the few provisions he had carried with him.

"My name is Dionysis Meletakis and I come here on behalf of Father Ieroclis from Cyprus. I came to speak with you and also to fulfil a promise that I have given to Father Ieroclis; to bring you a message. Here it is," and Dionysis pulled out the envelope from his inside pocket and gave it to the venerable father.

"Father Ieroclis told me that he would inform you by telephone that I was coming," and instantly silently wondered: 'How could a telephone exist here, someone must have been notified at the monastery and came to give the venerable father the message.'

"I know who you are, my son, I have been waiting for you, I knew you would come. You chose a good time to come too, on Saint Demetrios's day, according to people's calendar, he should be honoured. As you may know we follow the old calendar and we are thirteen days behind. Come, sit down and keep me company, let's befriend each other. I have a few nuts to offer you and some *Tsipouro* that I save for special occasions."

Dionysis now had the full picture of the room he was standing in. He hadn't seen the old water tank and the sink that you have to fill with water as needed depending on how much water you consume.

'It's like the sinks they used to have in villages in the olden days,' thought Dionysis. There was another division further aback which looked like a small room. Then his attention turned to the venerable father. Venerable father literally means respected or spiritual father, it doesn't have anything to do with age. Of course Father Vonifatio must have been around sixty-five years old. His hair had thinned out quite a lot towards the front and had turned white, while his face looked much younger than his age. His beard wasn't that long but it was grey and his eyes light brown.

He was quite tall and skinny, the handshake of his pink hands revealed a hardworking man and his glance revealed a clever man, spiritually cultivated. The sense of his spiritual cultivation was more of an emanation of the picture of his face, his smile, of the peacefulness this person spread round. Dionysis had found out the venerable father had come to Mount Athos about thirty-five years ago and had retreated to his hermitage for about seventeen years now. It's perhaps difficult to understand these decisions for the human mind that has been taught to think in a worldly manner.

"Yes, my son, I have been here for a while now and whatever you see here serves its purpose," continued the venerable father as he answered a question Dionysis had thought of asking. "I read, I pray, I speak with God and I serve him."

Further down there was a pitcher, which obviously the venerable father used to save drinking water in. The room was poor and sparing but well-made and its physical location protected it from the winds and rain. Here, the venerable father had moved away from the profane and prayed for the world and the people he had left behind. Each one of us serves the world from a different perspective. The venerable father had followed the monastic life and then isolated himself even more to pray and serve God. This cannot be accomplished by just anyone; it's not easy to become a monk, to become a saint.

If a secular life or marriage amounts to climbing up a mountain, monasticism amounts to climbing up an abrupt, steep and higher mountain, and a monk, who isolates himself and lives entirely on his own, is climbing a mountain that is almost vertical. Dionysis sat there thinking about these things and others, contemplated by Father Ieroclis's words and their endless conversations that came about once Dionysis asked questions which had tortured him for a long time.

These questions revolved around Christ, about his human side and not his divine one. He wondered about Judas, a student and friend of Christ, and whether his betrayal could have been avoided or if it had to happen. Was Judas merely a victim of a course already erased? What did Christ do during the early years of his life, why should orthodoxy be the only correct theory, was God maybe not only one, regardless of how each of us worship Him? Isn't it perhaps the virtues and teaching that count? Are there perhaps other gospels or have things changed as the years have gone by? Or even, if God punishes, does he seek revenge too?

Dionysis remembered a couple of religious texts he had read when he was younger that inspired fear rather than faith and respect. Fires and hell for the immoral, or for whoever was different. How could all these things be just? He thought of other things that confused him. With the passing of time, many things cleared up in his mind, many things moved in place. He started praying more substantially, to love God more deeply, finding peace via God and his spiritual father, Father Ieroclis, this humble, bland man who belonged to the category of good clergy.

For the third time, he felt that the venerable father was a step ahead of him. First, he had told him that he had expected him and then acted as though he could read his thoughts. He couldn't hide and he liked that feeling, he felt relieved. He was even more relieved when he sat down with the venerable father and they talked and became friends. Dionysis told him everything. And when his tears started overflowing, as he spoke about his children, the deep wound in his soul and heart simultaneously, he started healing, gradually.

But something else was troubling him and, in the end, he couldn't help but ask. "Father Vonifatios, we have been speaking for such a long time, you don't know me but you were expecting me, you know what I'm about to tell you. If I forget to say something, your gaze helps me to clarify things in my head, but even though I brought you this envelope from Father Ieroclis, which probably says a couple of things about me, you threw it on the table and didn't even bother to open and read it. If you want to read it at a later stage by yourself and I'm just being indiscreet, then I apologise, even though I came all this way for this letter."

The venerable father smiled cunningly but with understanding and asked.

"Only for the letter?"

"No, no, I *wanted* to come but there was also the letter, the promise, the responsibility."

"Then the intention was accomplished," said the venerable father and, reaching for the envelope, he ripped it up into little pieces. Seeing Dionysis's surprise the venerable father continued.

"There is no letter, my son; the enveloped contains a blank piece of paper. You will fill it up here with your experiences from Mount Athos and our humble conversation. Father Ieroclis wanted to make you come to Mount Athos, to our monastery, to my poor hermitage, to help your soul heal and I think he succeeded."

Dionysis remained speechless but understood nonetheless immediately, and a wave of gratitude and love for these two people who led him to the peacefulness and greatness of Mount Athos submerged him.

Their conversation continued as they went into more depths about divinity. Dionysis spoke, the venerable father listened and then spoke allegorically back to Dionysis.

"They say," said the venerable father "that an eagle is condemned to die in ten years because its beak grows so much that it can't pick up its food to eat. And that's when it makes its big sacrifice. It picks up speed, high up in the sky and reaches lightning speed towards the ground in order to hit its beak and break it into pieces on the rocks, because that is his last hope, if he manages to survive, not to die from hunger.

"On most occasions, it doesn't manage to survive. But if it does succeed it comes out a winner, wiser and stronger. This is also implied in the psalms that you often hear, my son, in the divine ceremony…

«Ανακαινισθήσεται ως αετού η νιότης σου» which translates as *your mind and body are reborn just as an eagle's is*.

"And you have now achieved, regardless of your mistakes and pitfalls, ethical or not, to survive and you have to work on what is good for you and those around you."

Dionysis listened and treasured the wise words. Even if it was something he didn't understand immediately, he remembered it later on and worked it out in his mind. Father Ieroclis had taught him not to forerun and have patience. He thanked and kissed the hand of Father Vonifatios and the venerable father hugged him.

"Go my child, and may God be with you. You must always work for the good, with gaiety, with truth, faith and love. You must always hope and believe in God and you won't get lost. The magic of divine justice and love is beyond anything that man has created, which on the contrary will probably lead you to fears and uncertainties. Come now, go, before night falls, go with my best wishes…"

PART THREE

The Study of the Mystery of Death

"Our birth is also the beginning of our death. Throughout our course in life, the closer we come to God, the calmer and more peacefully and beautifully we will come to accept death. During our lives we pursue material goods, we collect money and experiences. All these, will one day disappear, we will rest and we'll leave on a big trip and everything else will stay behind.

"Some will take our fortunes; some will be called upon to decide on what to do with all the objects we have collected over a lifetime, things that initially awoke or created so many memories in us, even the smallest items: a cut-out from a newspaper, a photograph, a telephone number, a note...important stops in our lives.

"The objects will eventually be scattered around, unless we manage to transcend this passion, this nostalgia and love for old objects to someone else who will then regard these as sentimental value, our children or grandchildren perhaps. And if these people continue to assemble these objects, a museum of time will grow until the duty is given to others further down the line.

"We only pass by in this life, a meaningless star within the millions of galaxies. Whatever we have assembled in our mind, heart and soul, learnt or not throughout our life, everything will stay behind. Thoughts, virtues, ideals, which, without thrift, we leave behind for the many, for those who follow. Mostly we leave these behind for our people and family who are lucky enough to be left with our material and intellectual goods and who will use them to play the game of life, to experiment, using our values as a compass or our professional knowhow, as ideals for a happier world.

"If we smile on the day we die, if a part of our soul has remained pure, untouched by the syphilis and the decay which has threatened us throughout out trip, we keep a harmony, as animals, plants, flowers, insects and the whole of nature does, then we can say we have reached happiness in our lives and success.

"A great person once said: "What is important is to take part in the game, to be a player, to make mistakes and move on," and "Don't sit on the side and judge."

"We all collect and save things, we make our fortune and that makes us happy. But the biggest fortune is found in our minds and soul. Thousands of images, words, experiences, mistakes, whatever we bequeath as values and pass on to the ones that follow; whatever represented us, either openly or anonymously.

"I have always kept objects. Insignificant little things, as I mentioned above, heirlooms of my parents and grandparents, thousands of memoires from the depths of time. Once in a while, I liked to sift through these, to look at them, to stroke them, to look after them and, my worries would turn into what would become of them when I eventually left.

"Thinking of all the aforementioned, I simply decided to be a good player, to transcend a couple of the things to the ones who would follow the best way I could, to be freed from the stress and think with happiness. And something else…to write, to talk, say how I feel, to transfer my beliefs and values on paper. Only then did I start calming down, thus leaving something palpable as well as conceivable behind. I want my remembrance to be a good one; for the person who thinks about me to do it with a smile, with internal rejoicing.

"Our leader in all this is God. He will accept us in the end, he will measure our soul.

"But now my friends, I have to say goodbye. It is time to go and find my companion, my wife who left this world so soon. I must meet her, get together again. I honestly leave with a smile, because my son and my grandchildren represent everything which I have spoken to you about. And so I part calmly and I love you."

Father Ieroclis spoke his last words with deep pain and with superhuman efforts. The old man Nicolas, his friend, Dionysis's father, had died and he had directed the funeral himself in Limassol, at the" Ayia Triada"(Holy Trinity), the church that Mr Nicolas loved more than any other.

The church was a majestic place with a courtyard in a very quiet quarter, in the heart of the old town, close to Ayios Andreas Street and the Municipal Library. It had been standing there for years now amongst the huge palm trees and other trees which rose along the lengths of the courtyard on the southern but mostly on the eastern side. On the northern side two little houses neighboured the church, where two vicars lived, the two priests that Dionysis, as far as he went back in time, remembered being there forever, as if time had not touched them. On the western side was the main entrance.

In the church, and while the bells rang slowly but loudly one could hear the funeral's tone of sadness and departure at regular intervals, people stood under the big dome, with the echo of Father Ieroclis's words who had just read his friend's speech, still ringing in their ears.

His last wish had surprised everyone. Instead of letting them speak out some 'goodbye' words, he told them that he had written a speech only once in his simple and honest life and had asked his friend, the priest, to read it at his funeral. He also asked him to give Dionysis and his grandchildren his text book with his poems. The people, who were obviously touched by this and out of breath, listened to the words of the old man Nicolas.

Dionysis cried, but at the same time, felt good because he had managed to see his father before he passed away. Father Ieroclis had told him that his father wasn't well and pleaded him to come. Dionysis booked a ticket straight away; the time had come for him to return to Cyprus. His father lived for another four days and they said a lot to each other, but only when the unbearable pain of this horrible illness allowed him to do so.

When he felt a little relief with the help of morphine, the two had the opportunity to talk. Nicolas had even asked for a cigarette. He insisted so much that Dionysis had to give him one.

They talked about many things but it didn't seem enough. That's why it's best to spend time with the people we love while they are well because at some point they will go and it would be horrible to not have had the time to do or say the things that we've always wanted to. A thank you, and I love you, an apology perhaps. This is what Dionysis was thinking of, these thoughts raced through his mind at an impressive speed, along with mixed feelings of relief due to the fact that he managed to see him one last time before he died and that the old man was redeemed. He felt joy for having had a good time with him even during his last painful moments and pain because he had lost a good friend.

He thought of this like a lost soul, as people passed by him to give him their condolences, and simultaneously all these things that he had kept inside him for all these years overflowed in the form of thick tears that descended his face and cleared him from all of this like spring water…

Suddenly he saw her, three seats behind him, awaiting her turn; Cleo, his ex-wife, a changed Cleo, always beautiful, a little tired but more humane. She stood opposite him and their eyes met. Two people who had had two children together and had lived together many years, two people who perhaps never entirely understood each other but knew a lot about each other.

When you live with someone for so many years you inevitably see them at their very personal moments of craziness, anger, love, sex, joy and sadness.

"My condolences Dionysis," said Cleo holding back a sob. They hugged, a hug that 'rubbed-out' a lot of things…he kissed her and quickly whispered in her ear, he wanted to take the children and go out one evening before he left for Thessaloniki. These moments of unselfishness and off-loading help you do things that throughout a lifetime, due to bitterness, anger and egoism, perhaps, you cannot contemplate doing.

And at that moment a window opened for a family, a couple who had ended their relationship, to at least be friends with each other. They owed it to themselves and their children.

The old man Nicolas always visited his daughter-in-law, he had made sure to make a last gesture…

A True Friend

"Limassol, my Limassol, you are the most beautiful city in the world," says an old song and Dionysis repeated it in his mind and believed it.

The town he had grown up in, where he spent his childhood's most innocent years playing, not in front of computers and computer games but in the side streets and in the fields playing football, marbles and hide and seek. Even though what he missed the most from Cyprus were his children, the second thing he missed the most was his home town. Not so much the people but the city itself. Its old districts, its heart near Athanasiou Diakou Street where he grew up, next to the" Ayia Triada" church.

The old water reservoir which stood, and still stands, in the centre of town opposite the central police station, which looks at the town from above and watches it stretch out like a spider's web in different directions, especially towards the hills where the fields and dirt tracks have given their place to new districts, replaced by luxurious mansions. Progress or vanity really, development…or something else…

The 'Iroon square', the only square in Cyprus that reminds one of Athens, and which, initially, hosted bars with a bad name and night life, now, and during the past couple of years, has cleared up gradually and local taverns, revamped buildings and coffee shops have started popping up here and there.

The Municipal Library, a beautiful Venetian-style building with huge gardens and trees around. With nice stone ledges, brown windows and huge tall rooms, used as a library and also hosting exhibitions and cultural events.

The Municipality close to the market, the Governmental Administration building on Anexartisias(Independence) Street, one of the busiest roads with many shops. The "Tourkomahalades"(Turkish neighbourhoods), which started off at the "Tessera Fanaria," a bridge that was lit up by four tall lights. Truly, there were so many things, details, roads, buildings and reference spots that Dionysis loved and which reminded him of so much.

Now sitting on a wooden bench by the pier, on the big wooden dock at the old harbour, he thought about all of these things. After about a forty-minute walk at 7 a.m., and the ordeal of his father's funeral, he was now sitting near the sea taking in deep breaths and surveying the sea to his right, the fishing boats, the entrance of the old harbour, and to his left, the ten-kilometre-long beach road, the hotels and the city, which was slowly waking up on this clear, spring day.

The seagulls were flying here and there, they dived, touched the water, then rose up again; they came to shore and then set off again towards the deep waters while many fishermen along the dock fixed their equipment, talked a little and took in the fresh sea breeze.

They say that the sea and the sound of the waves, from time to time, can be slightly deafening, like an orchestra of percussions, which is miraculous. Relaxing you, they sink in, detoxify, solve troublesome thoughts and give energy.

That's how Dionysis felt right now. Yesterday was a hard day, old man Nicolas had gone forever. After the stress of the past days, he went to bed early and slept deeply. He slept early and woke up early and found himself here, now in his tracksuit, refreshed and capable of sitting and contemplating. He enjoyed the symphony of percussions that the waves created, the fishermen, the image of the city, the remembrance, the people and things he was deprived of, all these years, their lack of which, reminded him of how precious they were to him.

He had agreed to meet for coffee with a friend, close to the castle, the old castle that was only two minutes away on foot from the old Limassol harbour. We often say old harbour because many years ago a new one was built, a bigger one on the west coast of the city. There, commercial boats and ships came in and out with a big inflow of imports and exports, even though during the past couple of years a decline had been noticed since other commercial destinations were found in the region that obviously were of more interest.

Dionysis got up and started walking towards the square of the castle to meet with Costas. It was nearly eight o'clock and he found his friend waiting for him, sitting outside the quaint cafeteria with the house of Richard and Berengaria, a residue of their empire on the island as a background.

The two men hugged each other and kissed, even though a few hours earlier and later at Dionysis's father's house they had been together again drinking coffee that Ms Kallistheni had made for them. She was old now but fine; she looked after Dionysis as though he was still a child, just like when he used to come home from school hungry or with a bloody leg. Yesterday though there were a lot of people around them. Now, the two friends were alone and they wanted to speak from the heart.

The last time they had had the opportunity to do this, if you disregard some frequent telephone calls, was the day Costas took Dionysis to the Monastery of the Fools and then to the airport. They said a lot. They spoke about Thessaloniki, about Mount Athos, their jobs, the monastery, about Costa's promise. They spoke about Dionysis's father, about their children…Costas assured him that he kept his promise but they didn't say anything else about that…and left it at that…

"How is Nefeli, Costas? How are the children? Both of them must be little ladies by now. How old are they now? Eleven and seven?"

"We're fine Dionysis. Nefeli…(and his face lit up) is always well. We love each other dearly as you can remember. We are made for each other. I'm the monogamous type, you know me. Nefeli is my other half. We move on together steadily, hand in hand. And you know something Dionysis, I feel happy, because I may not have had as many experiences as I could have had with women but with my wife, we have lived such special moments that many who have met many women may not have been able to experience, ever. No, no, we are well, only my eldest daughter, Laura has come up with a small bump on her back and we are a little alarmed."

Dionysis was shocked.

"Oh come on, you're a jerk. We've been speaking all this time, you've been asking me so many questions and your daughter has a problem, and now you tell me?"

He felt horrible. How did it escape him, how did he lose himself in his own troubles and didn't realise his friend had problems of his own?

"Come on; don't be like this, you buried your father yesterday. I was waiting for you to calm down and then tell you. We noticed it about ten days ago and we took some tests, some specialised examinations. I hope it's nothing serious…"

Costas spoke his last sentence with a tremor in his voice and Dionysis grabbed his hand and squeezed it hard.

"Don't worry, everything will be fine, you'll see, it won't be anything serious; people like Nefeli and you are very well looked after by God, so that you can look after us who make mistakes."

He squeezed his hand even harder and Costas nodded affirmatively, deeply moved…

What everyone hoped would not be bad, thankfully it wasn't. It was a small benign tumour which, with a little medication, would dissolve by itself. Dionysis ran and found a friend of his who was a doctor in a private clinic in town and got a second opinion; he called a well-known doctor in Thessaloniki also and sent him the magnetic tomography electronically, for another opinion.

Costas, good Costas, who thought of everyone, was relieved, his face lit up. He took Dionysis to the airport once again and thanked him for the few days that he had run around for the wellbeing of his daughter. The two friends said their goodbyes once again.

Dionysis was happy to have been able to do something for his friend. He said goodbye to Ms Kallistheni, his children and then he left. He left after making sure he saw Cleo again for a drink, and only after he had accomplished the promise he had made to himself, for the four of them to go for dinner, Cleo, the children and himself; the whole family together.

Family Harmony

In the theatre of life, the protagonists don't have side margins for many rehearsals in order to be perfect. The present is written only once; the next moment becomes the past. What happens does not reoccur, and we all learn from our mistakes, or from the things we never dared to do from fear. Of course it is preferable to make mistakes because, when the time of assessment comes, it's better to look back and see a life full of experiences, with ups and downs and mishaps, rather than looking back at an empty life due to being scared of living it, just in case we make a mistake or even, get hurt.

Without seeking to, in our course of life, we use others as guinea pigs and others use us in the same way. We make many mistakes throughout the movie because we play our role for the first time and after a long time the same movie is filmed again, with us as protagonists again but with new people beside us. Then, the first rehearsal that has made us wiser leads us to handle things a little better.

An endless chain. A chain where one learns from the other. The chessboard is very big, the players each act for themselves. Apart from those few who think more of the whole of mankind. As people progress however, these become less, the anonymous heroes who knowingly lose because they think of the whole. And thus don't look after themselves enough. But it doesn't bother them because in the game of life they lead, victory doesn't count. Their victory is given by God. They feel good, they sleep sound, they have a calm soul and faith, hope and love towards their fellow man.

Dionysis and Cleo didn't escape the circuit. They learnt the hard way. He was oppressed in family businesses with

Cleo's father as a supervisor, he never felt as though he had accomplished anything by himself. She was young when she met him, spoilt and demanding. They both tried, they really did, they gave everything to their children, but year after year they drifted apart. Their love burnt out, love was there but that wasn't enough. They fought a lot; she would provoke him, never gave him credit for anything, and didn't understand him. He didn't respect her, looking for temporary happiness in other, foreign embraces. These were only strangers to him of course, but they housed balsam in his wounds and courage to carry on,so he thought. For the kids mostly but for Cleo, whom he still loved, only that she didn't fulfil him anymore; he didn't like her character.

Now, a few years later, and two days after his father's death, both Dionysis and Cleo were sitting in a cafeteria drinking coffee. If an outsider looked at them he would think that they were the best of friends. They couldn't remember how much time had passed since the last time they had enjoyed each other's company so much. That's how man is; full of oxymorons, his soul is an abyss. They say that God settled everything wisely and still the world is filled with so many paradoxes, absurdities, so many contradictions, which are inconceivable! Filled with imperfections. Full of ugliness. But that's exactly where His wisdom lies, there with the imperfectness with which everything functions, that there are no two people in the world that identify each other fully and each one of them, every time, reacts differently.

As they sipped their coffee they decided to take another step towards peace and take their children for dinner.

'Things are better, the little one will have his whole family united tonight,' thought Dionysis, 'everything falls into place with a little patience, with tears, with hope.'

They talked about so many things, they even told each other jokes. Maybe old man Nicolas acted positively. They would never be lovers again, husband and wife, and as a couple they didn't match, but they could try to be friends. Dionysis asked about Cleo's father's company and found out that Cleo had started working there. 'Finally,' he thought, 'she has decided to make her own money the hard way and the change is obvious. She left shopping and friends behind, the gossip and the endless walks and the aristocratic behaviour.'

He found himself feeling bitter when he remembered all this; Cleo noticed this and asked why. Dionysis, laughing, told her what he was thinking.

"And how do you think I felt when I knew you were with another woman?"

"What do you mean when you say you knew?"

"A woman has strong intuition; she can understand a lot and at the same time hide things for years."

"And why didn't you say anything?"

"Because I preferred not to know officially, it suited me better that way. I was always defensive because I was insecure, you never managed to understand me or change me."

"You can't do that Cleo. Sometimes some things just don't work, they have an expiry date and we pester each other quite a lot as we grow older."

"You know, Dionysis, I think I can tell you now. I met someone, we have been dating for a while now and I have introduced him to the children. We are thinking of getting married."

Dionysis was surprised. After so many years, a feeling of possessiveness awoke in him for a couple of seconds, and then, after fighting with himself he felt happy. He saw a woman in front of him, his ex-wife, serious, changed, beautiful, and he was happy.

"Cleo, I wish you all the best. I hope that what I couldn't offer you, you will find in this new relationship. And I thank you for telling me, it honours me."

"And you Dionysis, how are you, don't you think about rebuilding your life? What do you do, how are you getting along?"

"I'm doing well; I have some simple, honest relationships from time to time. I never lie, I never promise anything."

"You will never change," she said.

"Neither will you," he came to the same conclusion, "we are all the same, yeast is always the same, we just grow older, we become better in some things, wiser. Other things we see more calmly, we just change costumes and our body gets older. But what we represent is always there, something is hibernating, sometimes it's thrown away in a corner but it's always there."

His mind went to Paulina and he smiled melancholically. The name Paulina, even though this woman had hurt him while trying to survive, was sacred; he put it in another category, he respected it, he never shared it with anyone. Not even with Father Ieroclis. Due to his egoism, he wanted it exclusively to himself.

"For example, you can't be romantic and suddenly be banal," he continued. "You can't get away, your fate always hunts you and what you have left somewhere neglected in a corner will at some point come out to the surface again and surprise you, it may even punish you."

They laughed, drank their coffee, spoke about their children, they made decisions about certain things that concerned them and talked about their meeting in the evening. Young Evgenios and Nicolas had been deprived of their father for a long time. That night they would not only have him in spirit but in flesh and bone too.

The Encounter

It was five in the afternoon, a beautiful autumn day. Actually it was the 17th of September. Costas was driving and listening to music, he was going to the Monastery of the Fools to fulfil his friend's wish for the sixth consecutive year.

He thought of a wise saying he had once heard 'It's not time that flows, but us that go along'. We're only passers-by in this endless eternity, an eternity of a few millions of years. Imagine, in a million years, what importance it would have if someone lived in Christ's era or in the 20th century. Now though, the difference is huge. If you take a watch and look at its hands for a couple of seconds, time will become synonymous with old age. Every second that goes by doesn't come back – we grow, the present becomes the past, and this repeats itself all the time.

At other times in our lives, some seconds seem endless while others go by and we don't realise it. They say that a dream only lasts for a couple of seconds but transports us to magical worlds filled with stories and faces, it creates combinations of people and situations which we don't understand and on occasion tell us stories without meanings... Then, at other times, you fall asleep and wake up a few hours later wondering what happened during that time, what you missed, what happened in the world while you were 'away'. How many people were born, how many died, how many fell in love, how many hurt, laughed, loved, hated. Time is an invaluable invention. We pass through it and it stands there as if it was our executioner watching us grow old.

What remains is what we did during all those millions of seconds that compiled our own lives. As a visitor we take a long course, the big circle of life, and then we get lost and give our place to someone else, a human relay race with no end. What we will do with the personal road we walked, what we will leave behind, what we will live and not what we didn't.

Costas and Dionysis were classmates in primary school. Costas was born into a wealthy family, but was not spoilt at all. They became friends from then. The one liked football, the other preferred athletics. The one didn't really like classical music, the other loved it. The one was born a leader, the other acted on a very low profile, nearly unnoticed. The one wanted to study civil engineering, the other history and political sciences. One a daydreamer, the other more of a realist, more grounded than the other.

What then bounded them together you may ask? The most important perhaps, was what I mentioned before. Their upbringing was such that it made them good people. They had the same values in which they fanatically believed. They consequently became friends and nothing else mattered. Everything else was secondary. They trusted and loved each other and supported each other in hard times. A poor child and a wealthy child who learnt so much from each other, they moved on parallel roads and managed, years later, to still share secrets and piously keep their promises, just like the one Costas had made to Dionysis.

Slowly-slowly, with these thoughts in mind, he approached the monastery. The now familiar place was more beautiful than ever. Suddenly all noise vanished and with devoutness he entered the monastery under a conceivable cloud, its gardens and woods. Costas could now hear different sounds; the birds that were singing, flying in and out of their nests, which they had built with so much love and effort, in the corners of the stone walls, in between the horizontal wooden pillars, exactly where the reddish old tiles met.

The scents were strong but not overwhelming. Nuns moved here and there like obedient bees devoutly going about their work. The queen, the abbess, who acted like anything but a queen, didn't give orders, didn't shout, wasn't snobbish. She was the queen though, she inspired a holy respect, she was humble but strict towards her faith, a strong person who had decided to devote herself to God.

Costas realised that during the past few years he had become a permanent visitor of the monastery , something peculiar had happened . The first time Dionysis had brought him to the monastery there were barely five or six nuns. Of course the monastery was small but it could host more people. Now he estimated that there were more than fifteen nuns and most of them were young. Innocent, bright faces of people who perhaps had a holy gift or a celestial calling that helped them choose their path.

He couldn't believe what he was thinking. "Is this me?" he reasoned, "me, who a couple of years ago believed all this was nonsense? A person who believed that these people were influenced by others, a person who was suspicious and saw everything with a critical eye." Not anymore, he wasn't fooling or criticising anyone. Religion is another world which, the deeper you get into, the more of what the philosopher Socrates said happens: you realise how little you know.

But now there seemed to be a change taking place, the churches filled, the monasteries filled up, people were reverting to God, to the Virgin Mary and the Saints, regardless of their beliefs about some priests.

"People aren't well," he reasoned, "saturation exists, a lack of ideals, it seems like we are moving towards a global disaster and the only hope we have, perhaps, is to turn towards God." Yes, since the first time he had gone to the monastery with Dionysis, he had started visiting the Monastery of the Fools more frequently. And since he had heard the strange story of the monastery, true or not, he began to love the place even more. Two years ago, when his daughter got sick and they had to carry out some tests, he went to the monastery with his wife in order to attain strength and to pray.

Today he had come to honour the promise he had given to his friend for the sixth consecutive year. He also came for something else, something that had tickled his curiosity.

That's why he waited for this day impatiently and he had decided to get to the bottom of the mystery.

He had been coming to the monastery, on the same date for five years now and he always saw the same face there. A woman in her mid to late thirties was there every year, stylishly dressed but, in a way, conservatively also, with beautiful expressive eyes. She lit a candle, sat in the church for a while, prayed at a specific icon and then she would go outside and sit on a bench where she would daydream. She appeared to get lost in thought and it was obvious that she was preoccupied by something specific.

A nun who seemed to know her interrupted her reasoning from time to time and after an exchange of a couple of words she returned to her own world. Then, she would leave just as she came, sweet and melancholic, leaving an aura behind that prevailed a human with duty, and a story...

The first time, he had hardly noticed her, the second time he saw her and racked his brains to try and remember where he had seen her before. After a while he realised that he had seen her there before, in the same spot. The third time, an idea came to his mind that before he reached the monastery he might see her again, but didn't make much of it because he thought that the coincidence would be too much and it was. The fourth time he made a bet with himself that she wouldn't be there and lost. The fifth time he surrendered to fate and waited for her. This year it was the sixth time and he was determined to speak to her discreetly, politely, without offending her.

He would approach her in a friendly way, neither erotically, nor to flirt with her. Anyhow Costas was a 'breed' on the verge of extinction, he was a man who, after so many years of marriage, was still in love with his wife and she with him. A happy couple. He just wanted to speak to this woman. Such coincidences don't happen often he thought to himself. There is something more to this, an interesting story perhaps...

And so, on that day, he had decided to solve the mystery. In a while, the unknown fool – he had given her a name that suited the surroundings – would enter the courtyard of the monastery. He let her head towards the church. He wasn't worried at all, seeing as he knew, like clockwork, what her next move would be. And, as he hoped, the woman came out of the church and sat on her favourite bench.

This is when Costas got up and approached her.

"Good afternoon," he said.

"Good afternoon," she reciprocated with a smile in a friendly manner. The surroundings allowed this friendliness because, when you are there, you are informally tied-up with others. Like brothers and sisters from a different mother or father who all meet under one roof.

"My name is Costas and I have been waiting for you, I knew you would come."

The unidentified fool was surprised.

"And I'm Paulina, but how did you know?"

"For the past six years I've been bumping into you, here, every 17th of September. Of course you could say that for me to have seen you so many times means that I have also been coming here every year on the same date. It's true; you may not have noticed me because you are always lost in your own thoughts. But I have seen you enough times and I would like us to get to know each other. It's worth meeting a person like you. For you to always come here on the specific date it must mean that there is an interesting story behind all this and for you to keep this ritual so piously means that you are a person with substance."

"Thank you for your kind words, I have given somewhat of an oath and I keep it, but allow me to notice that perhaps something similar is happening with you, or am I wrong?"

"No, you are not wrong. I have promised something to a very good friend of mine as well who, after his divorce left to go abroad and he hasn't returned since then, so I make this yearly pilgrimage. He prefers to see his children in Thessaloniki twice a year where he is now based."

Paulina appeared to be moved a little and Costas realised this. 'Is it possible,' she thought, 'that Costas is speaking about Dionysis? There are so many coincidences, is this a sign?'

"If you allow me to ask Costas, what is your friend's name?"

Costas was lost for a while.

"You know, it's not that easy for me to speak about the life and secrets of somebody else. Not to mention to reveal his name."

"Is his name Dionysis?"

Costas stood up. He went to say something but she continued.

"Yes, Dionysis is his name, it couldn't be someone else. That's him, and because he decided to move on, he sends you to this fated place. That's my Dionysis, a man whom I know so little, yet so well…"

She continued talking but Costas interrupted her.

"Are you the woman he told me about?"

"He talked to you? What do you know?"

"I don't know anything; all I know is that he has a secret, which he keeps deep down inside of him, that there is a woman in his life and that he wants me to lit a candle in this monastery for her and his kids every year seeing as he has decided to stay away for the moment."

Paulina listened to him emotionally and her eyes watered. After everything that had happened with Dionysis he still thought about her.

After all these revelations, Paulina and Costas started talking like old friends. And as usual, we sometimes open up more easily to strangers and reveal our innermost secrets and thoughts and let on to our inner selves. We don't ask anything from that other person, all we ask is for him or her to be a good listener, and that alone helps us. She sat and told him everything. Costas had the right to know. And whatever Dionysis hadn't told him due to respect towards Paulina, she told him. Then she spoke to him about her own life, about her decision to move to England three years ago after her husband's death.

She told him that she had promised to herself that she would go to the monastery every 17th of September and she had done so.

"Maybe one day I will find what I am looking for, maybe the fools will enlighten me," she said with some bitterness.

Then she found herself interrogating Costas about Dionysis. She asked him about everything and he dropped the suspense and spoke about his friend whom he loved so dearly.

He told her that they had constant communication by phone, that Dionysis didn't come to Cyprus but that he took his children to Thessaloniki and that once a year their grandfather accompanied them. Dionysis's father, with whom they were so close. But the grandfather had died, he continued, two years ago and that was the only time Dionysis had come to Cyprus for a couple of days.

He also told her about Dionysis's progress and that he soon became the top engineer in the company he worked for. He also told her how he then got on the administrative board. Four years later they had decided to take a huge step and start some projects in Albania. They had given Dionysis some shares and he came and went where the building and development was booming. In a country where, after a few decades and hard times, people and things started breathing, with a price to pay of course, the cost of big and sudden progress in which some benefit big time by stealing, and others get poorer and equality is diminished. But freedom is freedom.

Dusk had arrived. After so many years Paulina cried for joy and Costas looked at a woman who worshipped his friend. How life treats you sometimes…They exchanged numbers and parted cordially. Each took their path back to their daily routine. They knew that whether they spoke again or not, even if they lost track of each other they would meet again in the same place, in exactly a year's time.

An Incompatible Youngster

Yiannis left Cyprus for two reasons. Firstly because he wanted to follow his dream, to go and find his fortune, as they did in the olden days, during years of poverty or political juxtaposition, mostly believers of the left, or as heroes of fairy tales did, and secondly because he wanted to escape from a conservative family, a father who was a civil servant and faithful to the system, and an overprotective mother who 'stuck her nose' into everything. She offloaded her daily insecurities on her children and made dreams for them without even asking.

They were good people, always formal, they believed Cyprus was the best place in the world and that everything worked like clockwork. Of course they must have done something right, they had exceptional children. Only that Yiannis, or Yiannis Ayiannis as they called him at school, which was a play on words that they estimated represented his love and infatuation for Victor Hugo, wanted to become a writer, while Alkis, his brother was passionate about music.

I read somewhere that the overwhelming love of a Greek mother creates either slaves or revolutionists. Thankfully the two brothers became revolutionists. They loved their parents, they respected them, but they knew what they wanted from a young age. They kept the good elements of their upbringing in a middle-class family, and the rest they created on their own. Of course nothing is coincidental in this life. There was also a biological explanation.

The oldest son Yiannis was very close to his grandfather from his mother's side, named Alkis, who in his youth used to write verses and poems as well as many articles in newspapers of his time. He attained his love for books from his grandfather who started reading fairy tales to him at a young age and then, when Yiannis grew up, he referred him to interesting stories and books, he became his mentor. He helped him with his essays and they would go together to the movies (only in the beginning, then they started taking the younger brother with them too) and watched everything that Yiannis had read, on the big screen.

Alkis, the younger brother, on the other hand, was very close to his grandmother from their father's side who lived in the village and had an outstanding voice, which of course she never developed. It was unheard of for a woman from a village to even think of going to a conservatoire or even study music.

As the world was then, each era had its particularities which can, twenty years later, seem so tragically absurd, but we shouldn't judge or wrong anyone. And of course the two elders, grandfather Alkis on the one hand and grandma Aidona on the other, tried, as usually happens, to pass to their grandchildren, their two times children, what they never managed themselves. And they were quite successful, although, on their way they had to confront the parents of their grandchildren who, being city people and realists, believed that what they tried to teach them was both fantasies and dreams.

The parents themselves admired seriousness, the correct and conservative dress sense, positive sciences. Each of us learns as they can. The children had a better judgment, at least in what concerned themselves and, when the time came, they put their foot down and did what they wanted. Thankfully their parents, although they were conservative, nouveau riche with some dogmatic ideals, loved them and were democratic people who gave in in the end and let them choose what they wanted. The bottom line was that a degree in something, was better than nothing.

The youngest, who wasn't that young anymore, went to Athens and stayed there, he never returned permanently. He grew up suddenly when he had to admit to himself at the age of fifteen that he was in love with a male classmate of his.

He went through a rough time; in the beginning people didn't accept him for who he was, he became unsociable and abrupt, he even considered committing suicide. It was a shame for his parents and to himself. He only felt some relief from his grandmother's side, Manto who was nicknamed Aidona (from Aidoni, a singing bird), and his brother who always understood him. He also found himself through music; here, he felt some peace. Then came his first relationship, many secrets, many lies, a lot of stress and pressure. He went through all this by playing the guitar and the flute. And he was great at it, he started writing and composing his own work. Music was his only exit to the endless dead ends of puberty he came across, as well as the army which, he had to go through. And when all this finished, he left for Athens and got lost in the crowd. He gave himself to music with passion and came across love and Eros as he had chosen.

Yiannis on the other hand, the best student of his school, left for England where he studied English literature and philosophy. From Les Miserables and The Three Musketeers to The Dreyfus Affair later on, and the works of A. J. Cronin but also Greek writers whom, when he discovered, went crazy, he found himself in England attributing D. H. Lawrence and Oscar Wilde. The British Kavafis, as he later on referred to him.

Yiannis also grew up abruptly due to the weight of his brother's secret. Yiannis was stronger than Alkis and he stood by him.

"I can't feel what you feel," he had told him. "I like women, I adore them and I desire them, especially older ones. I understand you though."

He was only eighteen, what else could he have said. A true oxymoron phenomenon, men finding themselves at the height of their sexuality from eighteen to twenty years old, while women find themselves there at thirty. It's a paradox but it's true. How this works in marriages and relationships is something complicated to understand. He only said one thing to Alkis on a more serious note and outburst that distinguished him. "I was and always will be by your side; I love you, I cannot change what you are and what you feel, but I will tell you one thing. If I ever hear you underestimate yourself, or offend your own name and dignity with foolishness, you're going to have to deal with me!" He was serious and Alkis knew this. This was what their relationship was like; strong, fraternal, friendly, and human.

Yiannis was a counteractive and revolutionary type of person, he didn't reconcile easily. And when he returned to Cyprus he tried to hang on to something.

We've talked before about the pressure and the cunning solutions that were put onto him. But he resisted, he didn't succumb to conventions. He dropped everything and went to Athens two years later where he found his brother. The rest you know. Sometimes you have to go against everyone and everything, you have to go crazy in the eyes of people who have learnt to think and act in a specific way, in order to succeed.

He succeeded, and that was mainly due to himself but also to Erato, who supported him more than anyone else.

For sure, the Monastery of the Fools and the confession of the stranger was for Yiannis, one of his biggest stops in life. The next big step places itself about three years after this, a couple of months after he had arrived in Athens and was called upon by the name Erato.

His friends in the beginning were limited although Alkis was very well networked. He looked after getting his brother into the social life of Athens. And so Yiannis found himself hanging out with quite a lot of people, going out, meeting musicians mostly. They were good people, dedicated to their art. Sometimes you would see one of them with ripped jeans and untidy hair and ignored him and then when you finally paid attention to him, you would find out that he was the most interesting person in the world.

You could easily speak to them about many things and you could identify a way of handling life which was different, more spontaneous, with no agenda, they lived in the present, each day as it came. On many occasions, Yiannis drew on topics from these encounters and went into a productive period where his writing flowed well and he started feeling good about himself and his insecurities started parting, his confidence rose and it was a matter of time to find the opportunity to succeed in something. His brother continued his classical music lessons and at night he and some other guys found a job in a bar where they played and sang songs of another era. They sang songs of 'the new wave' as they called it.

They gathered a lot of people, the pay was satisfactory and the owner, Petros, was an honest guy. Yiannis became friends with him and on many occasions he would spend his evenings there for a drink, an idle chat, to think a little, to dream. His favourite night was Wednesdays, the middle of the week. The place gathered more people than on other weekdays, but surely less than on weekends. It was ideal.

He lived in a small studio in Pangrati, and his brother lived close to the "Siles of the Olympiou Dios(Zeus)". Eight months had already passed since he had settled in Athens; it was the middle of April and in a few days it would be Easter that came late that year. Spring euphoria possessed him and he didn't want to stay at home. At the same time Alkis had invited him to go to the bar that evening, as he wanted, he said, to introduce him to his friend, George.

"You will also meet the best voice in Athens, Erato," Alkis had said to him in order to convince him.

"She's our new collaborator that plays the guitar and sings although she is studying the violin, but, like all of us, she's also trying to make her living. She is from the island of Mitilini and as do all the Greeks, she came to Athens to follow her dream."

Yiannis wasn't listening, he wasn't paying much attention. His mind was stuck on a name, 'George'. The time he had been afraid of had arrived. As soon as Alkis said George and noticed a change in his brother's voice, he also felt his heart tighten. Because it's another thing to state that some things don't bother you, another to state some theories, to have an open mind and another to be confronted with the truth in the face, to live it. His brother wasn't going to introduce him to a friend but he would introduce him to his boyfriend!

'That's it,' he thought, 'My virtues and beliefs are there. Everything is a theory until it is tried out in reality, and only then can you tell whether it is a valid one.' Everything would be judged on that night, only then, when he would meet his brother's boyfriend.

Erato

The night was special. It was April. Spring, a beautiful night with a discreet chilliness, perhaps the last remnant of winter, and a breeze loaded with the fragrance of spring that smelt of hope.

At around 11 p.m. he arrived at the bar, and immediately ordered a double whisky on the rocks, while Petros, who saw him, approached him and welcomed him warmly.

"I haven't seen you in a while Yiannis, how come you remembered us?"

"I thought I would unwind a little; lately I've been working day and night to prepare a project for work. I also heard about this lady you have employed, Erato, and I thought I would do you the honour." They both laughed. At that moment, the lights turned down and the programme started.

His brother played the guitar and accompanied in singing. He set his eyes on everyone on the stage. He also knew Gregory who played the drums, and Elias who was playing the bass. But who was the serious and timid guy who was playing the synthesiser? Although he suspected the answer, he asked Petros.

"Ah, that's George," answered Petros, "a big talent and a composer. One day everyone will be speaking about him and I don't mean people of the night only."

Yiannis smiled. There he was expecting to encounter a crafty, arrogant guy, but he saw a good guy, it was written on his face. He was glad, and Petros continued:

"And of course, at the end of the bar are our ladies. Aliki, the pianist, you know her, and the other one is Erato."

Instantly Petros called the ladies to introduce them to Yiannis. Their glances crossed and they shook hands. Usually a handshake only lasts for a couple of seconds – there is an unofficial protocol between people about this. That specific handshake though, lasted a little longer than usual and it had a warmness to it. That's what Yiannis thought about later, when the young woman got up to sing.

Erato wasn't impressive at all. Pretty, simple, with a little makeup to bring out some of the features on her face slightly and a little lipstick on her lips. They didn't have the time to say much to each other, seeing as the song finished with an applause and Alkis had come towards them with George and the ladies had to get ready for their performance.

He had finally met George, this trial was over. His brother seemed happy, although he was also stressed about the result of this introduction. 'I'm not made out for these types of things,' he thought, 'neither do I agree, even though there is nothing to agree with, seeing as this is what God, or their hormones, chose to be their nature, this is what would make them happy.'

At that exact moment a voice hit him straight in the heart and brought him back to reality. It was Erato singing. He turned abruptly towards her, electrified, and saw her looking at him. Their gazes met for a second and it was enough to warm his heart. He brought his hand, with which he had shaken hands with Erato a couple of minutes earlier, to his nose and smelt it. The smell of hand cream and other scents around him bewitched him.

On the one hand he was enjoying the songs and her voice and on other he wanted the performance to end so that they could have a drink together. And they did. Without any unneeded flirt, without one wanting to win the other over. They spoke so naturally and humanely about different things, they stopped one conversation and took on another. They made each other feel comfortable. It was the first time in a very long time that he felt so warm and comfortable.

Later on, when all of them went to have some food in a night restaurant on Vathis Square and they all sat together,

Erato, Alkis, George, himself and the rest of them, he felt that he was happy. At that point, that photograph in a snapshot, he and his brother, George and Erato, was pure happiness. He could finally see the light at the end of the tunnel.

For Yiannis, Erato was one of the most beautiful chapters in his life. They kissed for the first time two weeks later, when he accompanied her to her apartment once more on a Wednesday evening. It was Holy Week and the bar she worked in was closed. He had proposed to go together to church in Kipseli in the district where she lived. Being an island girl from Mitilini, she loved Easter and what it represented. The two weeks they had spent together were full of joy and jubilation. Their encounter, Easter that was approaching, the spring air and the hundreds of things they shared provided them with euphoria. They would start speaking about a subject and there when you thought that the conversation had come to an end, two other subjects unfolded.

After the service of Good Wednesday, they went to Fokionos Negri for a coffee and then to eat something in a tavern. That night was even more beautiful as well as melancholic. For those who believe in it, the Holy Week seemed to sympathise with the entire nature and lived events moment by moment, which had taken place two thousand years before for the crucifixion of Christ. The sky, the clouds, the atmosphere, the gloomy weather and the people. During those days a kind of truce seems to take place. Everyone brings out the best in themselves that they had hidden 'on the side', in their routine, in stress, pressure of survival, in the jungle of the capital.

They reached the entrance of the apartment block and there they kissed. They had held back for two weeks and now they both wanted to. Just a kiss, with the moon accompanying them. A kiss and a good night.

"I don't want somebody to tell me that they cannot live without me. I want somebody who wants to live with me."

That's what Erato told him. Something nice, with a lot of truth. Love, a word so often used by people who are never actually sure of what it means. Especially between man and woman, or between a couple. When you say that you love your children or your parents, or a friend, you rather know, you feel something strong inside and you know what you mean, the feeling is roughly the same with all people. The love of a mother, love towards parents. Love as in the 'bow and arrow' of Eros however? What is it, what is it based on? Can a feeling so great and undefined be based on something?

Each of us perceives and understands, everyone thinks differently, people are different between themselves, there are no two people alike in the world. The chessboard is huge and each one of us moves along between the squares and tries to find what they want. And most of us, on our way, get tired of seeking or we end up just settling and call *this* love; it may be just that, and we have the right to call it that.

Love is free, saying someone is yours sometimes sounds nice but it's a product of insecurity and it reveals possessiveness. Love is offered with no terms. You love a person because he or she has spoken to your heart, not because you expect something in return. Love is forgiveness, to accept the mistakes of others and to forgive − and doing so by giving back spiritual strength instead of weakness. I forgive you because I understand you, because we all make mistakes, because we believe in each other, because you are a good person and I believe you have learnt from your mistakes, that's what love is.

Love is the mixing of two soulmates, it's to go deep in the other's self, to be undressed in front of each other, getting one and giving two in exchange, but then getting back four in return. Love is what remains after Eros, if Eros is true…And Yiannis's and Erato's Eros was real. In any case, that's what her name meant in Greek (Erato vs Erotas). Erato was the name for Eros in the feminine form.

Erato stood by Yiannis as no other. The road to the top was difficult. When finally, he managed to grab on to something and collaborate with the publishing company, which he became a partner of at a later stage, and moved on together, he had to work hard. Erato was by his side, she never made it more difficult. But he also stood by her and her music, her studies. She adored the violin; she wanted to play in a symphonic orchestra one day. They moved on together and every day they would get closer and closer.

When Yiannis, being counteractive and sometimes nervous, would speak to her abruptly, she was patient and just answered him with a smile. A very difficult thing to do. And when she went to auditions and she had to prepare herself, he was by her side.

Time went by and Yiannis got better and better. He now had a job as a columnist in a newspaper. He had published some short stories, collections, and then his biggest recognition came through his book '*Witnessed by God and the Moon*'. The road was now open. The more he became acquainted with success, the more he loved Erato. He only hid one thing from her, the story at the monastery − Dionysis's story. He felt he had to keep it buried deep inside himself.

Anyhow, he managed to make the story known to others through his book, by changing names and some variants. Now they were asking him to go to Cyprus to be awarded for his work, to present his book, but also to meet his future collaborators of the advertising agency whose headquarters were in London and also had offices in Cyprus. He had to come in contact with the publishing company that would promote his book in England.

He had accepted the invitation; he wanted to see his parents, but also something else. He called Erato.

"Have you been to Cyprus before?" he asked her.

"No," said her sweet voice, "why do you ask me, since you know the answer?"

"Exactly," he said, "it's a good opportunity for you to get to know Cyprus. Do you want to come with me when we present my book there?" There was a pause.

"Yes, I'd like to if you want me to come, and as long as I'm not a burden to your work."

"What are you talking about? I'm booking seats and we'll talk about it more later on. You'll like it, you'll see."

"I know," she said, "but under one condition."

"Let's hear it."

"Next Easter you will come with me to Mitilini. I know it's too soon, we don't have to plan from now, it's best to take each day as it comes. But I want you to promise me that if all goes well, you will also come with me to Mitilini."

Things didn't go well, not well at all. What time doesn't bring, the hour does, a bad moment, as a great saying goes. Erato's brother, the youngest, Stelios, was killed in a car accident in Yugoslavia as he was returning to Greece, with two of his friends from Germany where they had gone to buy a car for Stelios.

He was the youngest of the four children, two boys and two girls. Erato was older than him by two years and they were very close. He was to come to Athens to work as a taxi driver with the car he had bought. He planned to make some money and see what he would do next...

He didn't make it though, his taxi fell in a 'death-race' in which he wasn't at fault, but the crucial thing was that the result was fatal. It's really amazing how these two words, Capital or Big City and Money, drain people; it makes them base all their goals on these two words. Everywhere in the world, not just in Greece. It's that unattainable a dream that it becomes a nightmare for most, and for others it becomes a nefarious circle, something like a cyclone from which no one can escape.

You go to the capital, the big city, you start off cowardly making a more comfortable life. Then you want a car, a house, a holiday abroad, a summer house, schooling and expensive clothes for the children and, although you are making enough money, you get loans also, you rise financially and socially, you get a second job to pay off your loans and you run spotlessly, filled with intensity, to realise one day that life has gone by. It has expired and maybe the things you wished for as a child, they are things that you made up in your innocent dream which never happened.

He left without a word, without a complaint, the only complaint was left behind to those who cried for him. "Why?" everyone asked rhetorically. As Yiannis also did, when, in October he went to Mitilini for the funeral. He wanted to be close to the inconsolable Erato who had lost her best childhood friend. At the funeral Erato let the violin cry for her. It played a wonderful sad piece of Bach that Stelios liked. Then her tears ran out. Her parents, supported by their children and family, accompanied their son to his last 'home'. They held his hand, kissed his forehead, and said their goodbyes. They looked tired, hunched and discomforted, as though they were holding, not the whole world on their shoulders, like Atlas did, but more than that, the unbearable pain of saying goodbye to your child so early.

It's tragic to bury young ones. There is something not right about it, nature's rules are reversed. The biggest rule though, that there are no rules, was a reality that everyone had to handle. In Stelios's remembrance? Each and everyone's lives, up until he would become a sweet memory after many years.

At his grave relatives and friends left many flowers. Erato left just one, as well as a small poem on his gravestone that would accompany him forever:

'*Death and life had a fight for you my dearest,*
And death won, but he didn't consider one thing.
Having you with him now,
you'll brighten up his home, so much that
he'll regret taking you.
Because he'd have lost the greatest fight
of eternity and immortality that God defines.'

Yiannis, that unfamiliar friend of Erato, that stranger on the island and in the family, was there, he went to the funeral and he cried. He cried for Stelios, he cried because he needed to, he cried for Erato's pain, he cried because it's natural to cry. Once upon a time we were children and we cried every day. But we all hide a child within us, even today.

And then Yiannis left as he came, without a sound and few words. He had a lot to do, he had to go to Athens to sort out his work and leave for Cyprus where he would have business contacts and meetings for his book.

He left, leaving Erato with her family, but he promised her that he would be with her in spirit. He left behind a lot of pain, which, everyone says heals with time, and others say that it heals because of the need for survival. Yiannis had now learnt that when someone goes at a wrong time, the wound is always open, you just learn to endure it, it becomes part of your life.

The Monastery of the Fools

Once upon a time, many years ago, there was a kingdom that was led by a very cruel king. This king was the eldest son of the good king who, unfortunately, gave the reins to his son, only to see his kingdom fall apart, a place where only liars would prosper, frauds, landowners that took advantage of the poor and its most humble nationals.

Within the kingdom, fear ruled, as well as injustice, and the poor old king sat locked in his room in one of the palace's turrets, unable physically to react. He was almost imprisoned, with little birds that would come to his bedroom window every morning being his only company. The little winged creatures came and went all day long until night fell, and then they would disappear to their nests.

During those years, there were rigid rules in the cities, rules that the few put in place, the powerful, and rules which suited only themselves, unjust to the poor, and to those who were different.

There were people who differed from others, people who dreamed, people who could, without being taught by anyone, differentiate between good and bad, black and white, day and night. And like we have, blind people and deaf people and handicapped people those were called the fools.

A fool was everyone who differed, whoever was incomprehensible, whoever was cleverer, and whoever had an opinion, whoever dared to speak out about equality and whoever was capable of thinking. The bad king had taken care of voting for a law which, according to it, whoever was thought to be a fool by the state, would be forced to live outside the town's boundaries, in huts, and would be obligated to help in the development and construction and would not be allowed to participate in festivities that the kingdom organised.

The fools were few, and slowly, they built their own village, at the foot of a mountain outside the kingdom's boundaries. They never tried to escape, never showed any disobedience. They would wait patiently for their duties to finish every day and withdraw to their village, only to concentrate on their thoughts, their studies, and their own worlds.

One of the fools studied mathematics, the movement of the earth, the change of day into night. Another was interested in the stars in the sky; others formulated inapprehensible sophistries, others spoke about the soul and others, about God.

A young lady, in her twenties, also spoke about God. She spoke about the saints and religion; she spoke about miracles and of faith.

Every night they would gather on a small square that they had arranged close to their huts and each took on the duty to present a topic. The rest listened carefully and asked questions as the night went by.

This is how two worlds were created, the omnipotent kingdom with all the wealth, the right of the powerful, with the unjust laws, the unhappiness, the misery and the gloomy faces of the people. And the world of the fools, with the calm and peaceful faces which smiled with joy. The first world was the strong and the 'free' one, the second was the weak and held the 'slaves'. Time went by and the fools were very happy in their own world and of course the other 'world' wasn't happy about this.

It was an evening in spring when everything changed for the worse. Ordered by the king, the small village was surrounded by soldiers who started throwing fire-lit arrows in all directions. The whole village became a huge burning candle and the fools ran in all directions in hope to save themselves. It was useless, no one managed to get very far and eventually they fell dead by the arrows, the spears and axes of the manic and brainless soldiers, the supposedly logical people of our story.

The old king had heard about his son's dark plans and the poor man didn't know what to do. He didn't see or trust anyone, but he had to find a way to help these people; his only friends were the birds which sat helplessly on his windowsill and looked at the old man sadly walk up and down. Perhaps they also realised that something bad was going to happen.

The old king sought for solutions with no avail and in the end did something that he had never done in his life. He kneeled on his knees and prayed. He cried, he begged to God, asking for forgiveness, and at the same time he begged to be transformed into a bird or an animal; to set him free. People had worn him out; the self-destruction, the hate, the ignorance and the intolerance.

Dawn had come; all that was left in the village were ruins, ashes and dead bodies. All the fools were dead. Apart from a young lady who was always dressed in black and who spoke about God, about miracles and faith.

She was rescued. She had gone out of the village that night to a small church that the fools had built for her, to clean it and pray in it. From where she was, she watched the disaster as it happened. She was bothered and lamented all night, she pulled her hair in despair. A huge wall, a jail, rose before her and she was trapped. She tried to escape, to run and turn her gaze to something else but another wall barred her path. Petrified she started hitting the walls trying to free herself; she ripped her clothes and scratched her body. In the end, exhausted, in front of the small church, she turned her gaze up to the sky and there where everything ended she saw a small window, a faint light, a flicker of hope that refreshed her and stroked her in an attempt to heal her wounds.

She saw God in front of her, transformed into the faces of all her friends who had begged her to survive. They told her that the entire field had been burned down, but that in a corner, a small plantation and its roots had escaped the fire and this very plantation was what would help the field be reborn. She had received an order, a blessing of duty. The young lady got up and survived, having reached her depths of despair. From then on, whatever happened, things would get better, all except the deep pain of the loss of her dear friends who had helped her soften up through the balsam of love, comfort and faith.

The next day at the palace, the guards took food to the old king and didn't find him in his room. He had exempted himself from his bonds and flown to the young lady.

She looked in front of her. Armed with holy strength she descended to the catastrophe and started collecting familiar items, beloved items. She got to work. She had to bury all the dead bodies and clear out the place. She then started thinking of the deed that God and her friends had given to her, and the vow she had so dutifully made: to build a monastery for them and herself.

You may know the myth of the Lernaean Hydra, a terrible monster which Heracles(Hercules) killed − one of his many feats. A monster with nine heads which, when one of its heads was cut off, another two replaced it. In this case, the Lernaean Hydra myth worked positively because, from the very same day, it was as though the catastrophe had brought a revolution along with it too.

The young nun had gained new allies. Two men and three women came to her and helped her bury the dead, they helped her clean up the mess and put things back in order. And all the birds of the forest got involved, as well as their leader, an eagle, their king. The old king, who sat under a tree at the entrance of the settlement, slowly built his nest. He sat, day and night, like a guardian angel of the young, small group which had been formed.

From that day on, whoever tried to hurt anyone or cause trouble to the society, they disappeared, vanished. The area and the monastery that was being built were covered by a veil, a white cloud that destroyed every bad or malicious act towards the holy place. The eagle was always there, an imperial and melancholic figure to which the birds were singing, and kept him company, as always.

The young nun became the abbess and was named Ilaria and died from old age, supervising the building of the monastery, watching while it was being accomplished, being filled with people, nuns and monks, people who prayed, she watched it become...a paradise. A paradise that accepted all fools who differentiated from others, who followed paths less travelled and people who paid for their choices with their lives...

They all listened to the history of the place in awe and such silence was maintained that you couldn't even hear the breath of the attendants, young *and* old. The first question was asked by a young girl, who was about fifteen years old, an age which you ask about everything and don't accept things easily.

"And why has the monastery only got nuns now?"

"Because, my child, when other monasteries were built, they separated men from women and the men left, they went somewhere else, to other towns, to other places and they taught the story of the fools there."

The second question came from an eleven-year-old boy.

"What became of the old king and the eagle?"

"The old king, as we said, became an eagle and sat on the edge of the monastery's boundaries and was a sleepless guard. The story says that whoever tried to do any harm to the monastery regretted it bitterly and was destroyed. The veil that covered the monastery protects it. The old eagle, when it realised that the sweat, tears, and blood of Ilaria had become a river that flowed and never returned, that the monastery was in no more danger, disappeared one day, just as it came. Some say that it went up into a high mountain, as it deserved, and died proudly, as the king that he was. He died at ease about the monastery but was melancholic about the toughness, vanity and bad judgment of his son and successor."

"And what did the kingdom become?" asked a young man.

"The kingdom was destroyed, as with all temporary things. People gradually started to attain an opinion; the fools started to multiply and fled here and there to get to know the world, to learn more, to create a better life.

"Those who stayed behind, who were the majority, got lost with their leaders, they paid the price for their ignorance, their superficial knowledge and their fanaticism. Others came and they dissolved them and the kingdom burnt out, it withered like a flower that has no water for a long time and which gradually withers and dies."

A cowardly voice in the beginning but more emphatic as it spoke, spoke out from the depth of the crowd.

"And this story, alone, is a true one or is it a myth or a fairy tale?"

As soon as Costas asked the question he regretted it, but he knew that he would regret it even more if he didn't ask it. He was a fine man and he didn't want to offend her.

"This story is what it wants to be for each one of us. It's something like religion, like faith. For someone to believe in it, he or she has to be ready to believe it. Some continuously study the Writings; others just believe it with no research. This here is something internal, this story is a deposit about life and each of us is entitled to research it and understand it as he or she wishes."

People started parting and the only one that stayed behind, deep in thought and still stuck to his seat, was Costas. When Dionysis left, Costas continued coming to the monastery not only because of duty towards his friend, but also because he liked it. He had given a promise that he had to maintain once a year, but he had also started searching within himself. Each one of us finds their spot and Costas came here every so often to relax, to pray. And today, a year and something after his promise, he was looking for the nun, Ilaria.

She had the same name as the abbess. He asked where he could find her and they directed him to a small room behind the church where her cell was located. It was December and he had come early that afternoon, before darkness fell; the weather was dull and rainy, and it was cold. Ilaria allowed people to visit her in her cell every Thursday; young, old, women and men from all crossroads of life.

On that magical afternoon Costas found himself faced with three big surprises. The first one was when he walked into the small, warm, dark-tinted room and came face to face with a nun dressed in white with an amazing, beautiful and peaceful face which was black. He hadn't expected to find a black nun, who spoke fluent Greek and who was loved in the monastery.

His second surprise was when he heard the story of the monastery, the fairy tale, or the legend, he didn't exactly know how to characterise it. Something between logical and illogical, a kind of fairy tale for small children with meaning though, that only people who were aware could grasp. That's also why his abrupt question came up, since he had never heard such a story before, and he still didn't know if everything he had heard was true or not. But that was of no importance because he realised that Ilaria spoke allegorically, she wanted to send out a message.

The third surprise came when everyone left and he remained alone. He went to introduce himself to the nun and thank her. Before he was even able to open his mouth, she spoke out to him and said:

"I have been waiting for you, I knew you would come, but you took a little longer than I thought."

How did she know, who had spoken to her about him, did Dionysis speak to her? Why was she waiting for him, what did they have to say to each other? He found no answers to his questions and he didn't ask her either at this time, he just believed. He believed in the gentle and bland look, in her innocent smile, full of love, and in her voice. They had a lot to talk about and before you knew it they became good friends.

When Costas was ready, the nun told him her story. She was the daughter of a Cypriot business man, Marinos Iliadeli, who lived for many years in Zaire and became rich. Her mother was black and worked for her father. A usual story, which every so often happens with protagonists who are powerful and suppressed women who work for a piece of bread. When her mother died (until then she had thought that her father was also black and that he had died in an accident when she was two years old), she came to Cyprus to meet the person who had given life to her, whoever that was.

Her name at the time was Marina, and she always wondered why, until her mother revealed her personal story to her, shortly before she died of tuberculosis. Marina, Ilaria now, cried bitterly; when she buried her mother as a Christian Orthodox she dedicated her life to the church, and poor people.

She became a nurse and helped sick children. Then she became a nun and, on various missions, she travelled to many African countries. In the end, and maintaining the promise that she had given to her mother, she returned to Cyprus and got into the Monastery of the Fools while, simultaneously, tried to find her father. Her father, when he saw her, was shocked and denied everything and turned her away.

He already had a family and had become someone, he couldn't let her move the calm waters which surrounded him. The still waters of his life. Her mother supposedly loved him and always helped him. When she fell pregnant, he turned her away because he thought that she had had another relationship with another man of the same nationality. It was natural, seeing as he wasn't prepared to make their relationship official. He thus turned her away by egotism and cowardice, he couldn't face the gossip.

Her mother never got married and told her the most wonderful things about her dead father. Marinos never found out that the child was his, because Ilaria's mother Mayia didn't want to be a burden on his path. He was very ambitious and he made it. Now, almost seventy years old, he lived in Cyprus, with all his comforts, his children and grandchildren. How could this nun suddenly, out of nowhere, come to find him and tell him that she was his daughter? This shocked him; he hesitated and told her to go away. As he had turned her mother away. Just like Peter who was strong and of whom everyone was scared but disavowed Jesus three times. This is how he hesitated once more.

First with the mother and now with his daughter. During the two meetings he had with fate, he failed. He preferred to do the 'right thing', not what he *should* have done. He married a Cypriot from Zaire, a good woman, they made a family, children, grandchildren and good fortune. What is the right thing to do, nobody will ever know…

Ilaria didn't complain, she knew that he was her father, she had her inside information. Her mother had given her a box in which her whole life and dreams were locked; Ilaria knew…

She returned to the monastery and never left ever again. Her life was there now. She only travelled on missions to Africa once in a while, and to her other homeland, Zaire, but to other places also and it helped her. She softened the pain of people, she was becoming wiser and then she returned to the monastery. And because we're all human, with weaknesses and sentimental needs, and Ilaria, above all was human, she revealed her story to Costas.

You don't understand a human being, says a wise saying, not by just listening to it talk, but also by the way it hushes. And Costas, when the time came, hushed and listened carefully. Humanity consists of millions of stories, short and long, and every one of us finds the person we need at the right time, to tell our story. And an endless chain of human stories is born, life itself…

Soulmates

Dionysis had it all. Or at least that's what everybody said. Usually that's how it happens. A lot of people see someone and want to be like him, because most people don't know what they want. As a result they are unhappy because they can never set their own goals – what they want, what they love or small perhaps, unimportant things, which would bring them happiness. They create heroes and in many cases, wrong prototypes. One of these prototypes for many was Dionysis. He wasn't a wrong prototype at all, but wrongly, people confused his success, his professional development, the money he made, with happiness.

They had invited him to a cocktail party of the advertising agency which he was collaborating with and he was now driving towards the head offices in the centre of town. Before he set off he had to pass by Aglantzia where his company was building a big complex, to inspect the recent progress.

He remembered when he first came to Cyprus from Xanthi in Greece, where he had studied, and was banging on doors here and there and submitting job applications. He was twenty-five years old then, and couldn't rely on his father for financial support anymore. Anyhow, when he was studying, he always found odd jobs here and there to support himself financially. Mostly he worked on weekends as a waiter, or for the last two years he helped out his teachers with their work and papers.

He made applications, and when he tried out one or two offices where the chemistry with the owners wasn't too good, he went to Nicosia, to the company of his future father-in-law and stayed. He became a city man; in the beginning he rented a room in the house of one of his mother's cousins who lived with her husband in Lakatamia, a suburb of Nicosia. They didn't have any children and looked after Dionysis as their own child and he kept them company.

Gradually, as things started to get better and he started making more money, he rented a small flat in Aglantzia and, as the years went by, he progressed a lot. As he passed by his old flat , everything he had gone through flashed through his mind. He recalled how proud he was of his flat with one bedroom and a small living room. It was so small compared to the house he had now, with all its comforts, a garden and a swimming pool and his office, his private space. 'So small yet so nice,' he thought, 'the first years, those of creation, when you try to grasp on to something and work hard. When you impatiently wait for a rise, the Christmas bonus, the summer holidays to let yourself go. When you have only yourself to think about, no family, no obligations, no nagging.'

He carried on driving with his thoughts for companionship, seeing as, as usual, he was going about his business duties alone. He thought of this bitterly. His wife rarely followed him anywhere if it had to do with work. She considered all these things as boring and monotonous, even though they were part of the duties of the company that she and her sister were shareholders in. Years ago, her father had founded this construction company and it soon picked up, and the company was now at an envious standard in the market. Dionysis was one of the best and most loyal employees of the company and he worked hard, his work was appreciated.

Soon, the young and spoilt daughter of the owner flirted with him and, soon enough, became his wife. He didn't know how to fool people and he was very proud regardless of the bad-mouthing around him, which stated that all he was after was a large dowry, as well as other gossip that did him no justice. He was a good person though and he soon won people over, even the distrustful ones. When his father-in-law had a bad cardiac arrest, all eyes turned on him. His sister-in-law, Areti, who was more down to earth and logical, trusted him.

His wife was more interested in the social status – that her husband was to become the director.

He loved her but he was a humble man who didn't take advantage of situations, and he believed he was ready for a permanent relationship, a family. When Cleo fell pregnant, without giving it a second thought he asked her to marry him. 'Maybe all of this was based on wrong estimations, wrong ideas,' he now thought.

He interrupted his thoughts and parked his car in the parking lot at the back of the advertising agency's offices. He got out of the car, locked it and headed nonchalantly towards the entrance. He also got tired of such events but he was prompt, he didn't ignore anyone, he was correct in his work and that's why they respected him, and everyone wanted to work with him.

It was the beginning of autumn, the 17th of September to be precise; he felt good tonight, he tugged at his jacket to straighten it a little, exchanged a couple of words with the guard at the entrance of the building as he usually did, and carried on inside the building where people had already started to gather.

He saw her from afar, to his left and he instantly felt a pinch in his heart, which initially, he hadn't realised exactly what it meant. She stood out from all the others, she wasn't the prettiest one there, but she stood out. She also saw him and she was happy that there was enough distance between them and that he hadn't notice her uproar. Paulina was wearing a red dress, simple, with a black jacket, or rather, something like a cape.

Her cape looked like a spider's web that waited to enwrap its victim. What upset her the most was that this idiot didn't even try to escape from her web. On the contrary, he grabbed a drink and headed straight towards her.

Dionysis wasn't a womaniser, but he had his charm and won everyone over with his attitude and good manners, which showed a person that was anything but a man who let things get to his head. He used his powers at work. He was a tough negotiator and played with honesty and frankness. He didn't accept hits below the waist though, like the one Paulina was preparing to give him.

He approached her and introduced himself, and she returned the gesture, coldly initially, as though she was telling him to go away and escape the situation, but then she succumbed too. After all, in one way or another she had to approach him, that's why she had come tonight. What was she thinking, it had to be done, and better it be done an hour earlier than later…

'The fastest I do this,' she thought, 'If I meet him and open up a communication channel with him, I will satisfy the clan and win some time. Until I see what will happen.'

She hadn't the faintest idea what her plan would be. She did know that she had to escape from a net that she had become tied in, and she was quite responsible for this. The key was in this businessman's hand, as they had explained to her and that did no good to them and to their work. She didn't know whose work; all she knew was the vagrant who had intimidated her.

Then again, what does 'intimidate' mean, was she a little girl? It took two to tango and she had consciously side-stepped, and the price was a heavy one because she had sinned, but also because she had also chosen the worst person to dance with…

Dionysis interrupted her thoughts when he asked her if she wanted something to drink. She asked for a vodka orange and regained her courage. She prepared herself to dance again. The bad thing was that she was expecting to meet someone who was arrogant, who would play the fool with her, who would speak about the company and his money and, she would think to herself, "whatever I do to you, you bastard, you'll deserve it". On the contrary, she felt even worse when she realised, and it didn't take her long, that a rare person stood opposite her.

They spoke while they were surrounded by many people, changing positions. Everyone came to Dionysis to say something, the directors of the company, other collaborators. On the other hand, Paulina had to speak with clients, share her time right. An invisible magnet pulled them together in the end though. And they ended up not speaking about work, rather they had started speaking about what tied them together; work, and used it as an excuse for as long as it was needed.

When, almost simultaneously, they changed conversation, they started talking about one topic and then jumped to another. You could see joy on their faces, they were having a good time. Although, Paulina knew that an invisible eye in the crowd was watching her, was noting her every move, someone who had an agenda, someone who wanted to cause harm.

There are people who, in a couple of hours, can exchange a thousand words and this was what was happening between Dionysis and Paulina, that night. And because it didn't happen in a provocative way, it wasn't commented on, if we set aside Mary who, from time to time pulled Paulina to the side and made fun of her. In good faith of course, supposedly she was talking to their most popular client who appeared to have a soft spot for her, and that she should take advantage of the situation, as well as other comments. How could she have known...They spoke about music, books, movies and another zillion things...They spoke about their families and their children.

They listened to each other with interest, true interest. It was kind of hard to speak about their partners, as it usually is in these kinds of situations, when two people, somewhere between flirting and reality, avoid speaking about their partners, but on the other hand do so discreetly to the person across them, so as not to be misunderstood. Or even, to maintain the prototypes, like a defence mechanism against the sinful thoughts that fill the air.

Both of their attitudes were measured. They knew that they had a serious person opposite them and they had to be careful. Also out of respect, they had to protect themselves. Because, even though Paulina was disappointed that, in the end, she had to deal with a rare kind of person, Dionysis thought that he had to deal with a real lady.

The night went on and the 'goodnights' were nearly in order. People started parting and it was now more obvious who was talking to whom. They had to keep up some protocols and Paulina made the first move.

"It was nice to meet you, Dionysis; it's time for me to go though. I had heard about you and I must say that I am happy to have met you in person. And my impressions are even better now."

"I'm also glad to have met you, Paulina. I'm glad to have spoken to you as well, our conversation was warm and interesting. I hope we meet again someday. It looks like we agree on many things."

The conversation was interrupted at that point for self-protection, and they each had their reasons. You cannot escape fate though. You may have a person by your side and not know him at all, while, on the contrary, fate can bring two people on the same path, in a big city. Even more with other people's interests at stake, despite Paulina fighting for the opposite.

Fate, destiny, kismet, meant to be, is implacable. And Paulina would find this out much later from her mother, when she would decide to run after her shining star.

They met again at the theatre; Dionysis with his wife and Paulina with some colleagues. They watched a play of a modern Carmen. Seated roughly on the same level, she was on the left side of the stage and he was on the right. The performance was excellent, as both of them felt when they saw each other. They discreetly glanced at each other throughout the performance, though not only once. One of the times their eyes met, Paulina felt butterflies in her stomach and Dionysis a wild joy which he hadn't felt in ages.

The next day he phoned her. Nothing was alleged, he just asked her about the performance. Without them realising, they spoke for twenty-five minutes. They exchanged mobile phone numbers and, in the first text message that Dionysis sent Paulina he wrote a quote from one of Coelho's books:

"When the universe conspires, anything is possible."

And she replied with a quote from Kundera's book, "the unbearable lightness of being". And so slowly-slowly they started exchanging messages to each other and one raised the other's morale…

They moved along with the words of Kundera, Coelho, Kavafi and Karagatsi. The four names that were pronounced and written with a 'k'(in Greek), and they called them 'the four Ks', but gradually they also started sending their own messages and thoughts, releasing their own worlds which were amazingly rich. And all this, always discreetly, without offending each other, without taking larger steps than they should…

Many speak about soulmates, others reject it entirely, what's for sure is that there is something in this world; something strange, something unexplainable that unites the souls of two people. I don't know if for each of us there is only one soulmate, or if we have many. Probably the second. There are people who communicate on different levels, who on many occasions we can't even imagine. The point is not whether there are many soulmates or one. The truth is that there are few people who meet their soulmate during their lives, for many reasons; due to distance, religion and other reasons.

The main reason though is that few even look for their soulmates. Few get into the pain of seeking. Seeking means hard work, labour, disappointment, isolation from others because they consider you are strange, seeming as if you are hunting chimeras.

Sometimes an easy life doesn't do any good. It's bad for those who want to create. It makes you rely on others and forget yourself in 'boredom' or a 'leave it for tomorrow' attitude. And if you try and get away or if you rebel, guilt comes knocking at your door. "I shouldn't complain, being healthy is what is important, we belong to the 10 percent of the world that have food, who go to school, who have good medical care, who have a house and other comforts, who even have money."

No law says that we shouldn't have ambitions and at the same time appreciate small things like mankind's best gift, that is good health. No law says that those who continuously seek within themselves are ungrateful . No law says that, if something bad happens to someone, the only way to stand by them is to have something bad happen to us too, or to stop the search for happiness because 'you saw what happened to that person'.

Society projects a lot of guilt and clusters to people, with a dose of truth though, seeing as you really must be satisfied with less and with what you have. But a person's soul doesn't work like that, especially the souls of fools, of those who differ. Their soul is greedy, it tries to find its salvation, its peace and travels continuously in the abyss, trying to find the light.

They say that the less you know, the better. You are happy in your own ignorance and that's not bad. But you can't have all people be the same. "All, is made with wisdom." This wise saying is found in the fact that the Lord didn't make everything perfect. He wanted man to have a mind, he wanted man with his own will, to make mistakes, to question, to improve this small world he lives in, in the universe that He "in wisdom created".

Dionysis and Paulina sought for this something, this soul that would nurture them with love, with salvation, with peacefulness. They were fools and they made mistakes. It's better to make mistakes than to sit on the side and do nothing.

Dionysis and Paulina opened unusual avenues between them, for both of them. This didn't happen in a day or two. Not easily either. They sent and received messages, and built a relationship which they hadn't sought for. It was difficult, they put together a puzzle in their lives, and every day, another new piece was put in place. Soon the first coffee date came. At Dionysis' office though, with work as an excuse. That's how they kept their roles, each their files in hand and their notes. "They found an alibi, not to justify themselves but to justify themselves to third persons.

The only cloud that floated above all this was the one that Paulina was trapped in. From their second telephone conversation, she took another phone line for them to be able to speak through. She might have been exaggerating, for she was suspicious of everything and she didn't want to make any other mistakes. And the oxymoron was that she wasn't thinking of her husband that much, she thought of vagrants. She wanted to buy time and in the beginning she told her blackmailer that she had had no contact with Dionysis because he wasn't interested.

"All men are interested darling, if it has to do with women. And he didn't give this impression on your first encounter. So you go out there and find a way, and forget about evasions. Otherwise you know what's going to happen."

When two soulmates meet, it's a wonderful thing. They know they are attracted to each other; the universe is conversing for them.

PART FOUR

The Comet – Destiny

East Finchley, six in the morning. A young lady, in her mid-thirties, walks out of her house, upset, sits on the entrance steps and cries. Dawn has brought the first light of the day and the humidity caresses the steps, the tiles, the trees, the atmosphere, everything. Just as the humidity settles and turns into tears of water that run down the windshield of a car or on leaves of a chestnut tree, Paulina's tears ran down her face. Her life ran past her like a roll of film from a movie that only lasted a few hours, as many hours as it took for her to read the highly talked-about book of the talented writer that her company now wanted to promote in the United Kingdom.

Yiannis, an anonymous person to her, came into her life in the most beautiful, detailed and representative way. She cannot believe the coincidence, the game of fate, the convergence of the stars, how this stranger could have known so much about her. For sure it was her story, not that it couldn't have happened to anyone else, life was full of such stories and, not that someone else couldn't have written a similar scenario, but Paulina felt it, she sensed it, she knew it was her story.

This author's book was about her and Dionysis and there was something that linked both of them to Yiannis, this new author who managed to get deeper into her own thoughts, so much so, that it made her suffer. He managed to read straight through her and Dionysis and that was wonderful. If she had to meet this person to speak about work and the promotion of his book, she would, but now she also needed to meet him for other reasons, she wanted to speak about herself and perhaps, look for the footprints of Dionysis.

In life nothing ends, some things return, hover above us like fairies until the right time comes around. Often we try to do something, we try and find a solution, and we do everything except that what we truly believe in. The solution only comes when it's time for it to come, then when the stars converge, when all powers of the universe create a battlefield for relief to come around, resurrection and peace, as good or bad as this may be.

Yiannis was now in Paulina's constellation and he found her in London and reminded her of certain things.

'Maybe it's time to look at things for what they are, straight into the eyes; maybe I should run after my dreams once more.' She was more peaceful now. Crying and the peacefulness of the morning in this nice district of London where she lived appeased her. She lit a cigarette, made a nice cup of coffee and sat on the doorstep once more.

Inside the house her children were still sleeping, insensibly she had a smile on her face. Opposite her, two squirrels were running from one chestnut tree to another. One went up the trunk of the tree and the other one followed.

The first red double-decker bus appeared around the corner. It stopped in front of her house and the driver waved 'hello' to her, a man from Pakistan, with a beard and a huge smile. Then a milk-man passed by and left two bottles of whole fat milk on her doorstep. Strange, this had been happening for so many years now but this was the first time she was there to receive the milk herself. Honestly, how many things happened throughout the world when people were sleeping. Each of us has their own role in this absurd theatre of life.

Paulina laughed loudly this time. Each day dawned for each and every one of us and this day certainly dawned differently for Paulina. She got up, had one last sip of coffee and went inside the house. She had lots to do.

In the end Paulina managed to convince her mother to come to London for a few days. After all, it was no coincidence that she worked and lived in the world of advertising and marketing. Convincing people was one of her gifts. Not to influence people into things they didn't want, on the contrary. She told her mother that the children missed her, she told her about her duties and the new project in Cyprus and that they would return to Cyprus together. She confessed that she also missed her, she even said that, since she was by herself, she didn't have to think much about coming over. She told her to pack her bags immediately and come; she and her friend Pauline also hadn't seen each other in a long time although Pauline always sent her messages and kept in touch with her. In the end Ms Orthodoxia was convinced and now the three of them were sitting in a beautiful small café in Kensington enjoying a hot chocolate and talking about this and that.

During the past couple of years, the cold weather of London had warmed up a little. It had attained habits from other corners of Europe. One of these was all the small coffee shops that opened up here and there. They had always existed, especially in trendy areas but they were more difficult to find. Now you saw people not only stopping at bars and pubs after work, but also stopping in coffee shops for a pastry and a cup of coffee.

She didn't reveal the real reason, why she wanted her mother to come so urgently. Nor did she say anything to Pauline. But she had to speak to them, she needed to. She had gone through this for enough years now, she had to look at them in the eyes and speak to them. Her destiny was sending her strange and mixed messages. Reading the book had touched her. Suddenly, the timing of events was coming to unsettle her. Timing, as the English say, can be one of the most important things in our lives, in all sectors. Like when they say that a comet, every so often, at a specific time, passes very close to Earth and we are able to see it.

That moment is unique and it will happen again, it says, roughly in another fifty years or so. If at the very time that the comet passes by the earth, destiny passes in front of you also, you have to do something about it, do it, without a thought, with no return. Then it will go away, it will pass.

Paulina wanted to speak to her mother and Pauline about this whole story; her story. It was at that moment, after so many years, that she was ready to do so.

"...so this is what happened and recently they assigned this project to me, to promote the book and suddenly I found myself in front of my own life. And I don't know what to do..."

She finished her confession while tears poured from her eyes with relief, just as she had felt when she spoke, more laconically to Father Ieroclis, from emotion and shame at the same time. She was speaking to two women who were older than her, two of the closest people in her life, who loved her, and yet she never told them her most beautiful memories. She was ashamed about this.

Moments of silence followed her confession, like an ancient tragedy − when the final exit takes place and the peak of the performance arrives. Everything froze, silence. It was as though everyone was initiated into the act, every frequent customer of the beautiful warm cafeteria froze too. You couldn't hear anything, a silence that held for three or four seconds.

Paulina, as she spoke, thought about the day she was enlightened and told Dionysis the whole truth. She saw the expressions on her mother's and Pauline's faces and didn't know what to expect. When her narration finished, she caught herself holding on tightly to the side of the chair she was sitting in and felt her veins tensing and her blood flowing in the roads, on bridges, in the side streets and the crossings of her own self, just as it happens in the chaotic circulation of London at peak time.

The two older women looked in each other's eyes with meaning and the first word was said by Paulina's mother.

"My darling, when someone is open-minded and sensitive, he or she can understand and forgive a lot. Even more so when you are grown up and you have learnt that the biggest rules in life are that there *are* no rules. Imagine then, when in front of you, stands your own child and you hear all these words from her own mouth.

"When I gave birth to you in London, the person closest to me was Pauline. During the couple of days I spent in the clinic, she looked after me and we grew very close. This doesn't happen to everyone. We became friends and its value shows now, we're sitting here having a coffee all together.

"At night, when I used to take you into my arms and Pauline was there and we spoke to each other, you would open your eyes and look at me in a way that I will carry with me all my life. It was a gaze that said a thousand words that multiplies the love and makes it last forever. I would tell Pauline how happy this made me. At the same time though, I would tell her that I wished you would have an easier life than the one I had, one with less mistakes. And because I would repeat this continuously, Pauline realised that something had happened to me and gradually she let me speak to her and confess to her just like you have done right now.

"The story was very simple. My parents had set me to marry a very good guy, but I wanted to fall in love. I fell in love with your father and I created a relationship with him. At some point I spoke to Gregory, that was my fiancé's name, and thankfully he left with pride. The war came from somewhere else though, it came from home, and I faced big challenges and fights. Your grandfather took a long time to forgive me, especially since I had fallen pregnant. For him, everything was about respect. And so I got married to your father at very short notice and at some point we came to London so I could give birth. We told people that you were a premature baby, born at seven months. Silly stories really, but sometimes the human mind works in funny ways.

"Gregory was my biggest sin, because I wasn't decent with him. But I followed my instinct, even though I was taking a huge risk. Your father helped me with this; he always made me feel secure and told me that everything would be alright. He took on his responsibilities and stood by me. Anyhow, you know the rest of the story. You had a very special relationship with your father. I know how close you were to him. He left early, but I believe he was happy.

"The only thing he always used to say was, even though he loved Demetris, he always felt that you weren't fully happy. What was I supposed to say? I knew that you were still seeking love and I wondered what would happen the day love would knock at your door. You see, we don't decide on these things…And I was always worried because I remembered your gaze in the clinic in London, when you were born that had brought us together forever."

"And sometimes she would call me and tell me everything," Pauline interrupted, "and I would listen to her and reassure her, I couldn't do anything else but that, and be a good listener. I told her not to worry. She would tell me that sometimes she would see you as a withering flower that could only be freshened up by love. On other occasions she felt guilty because she pushed you beyond your capabilities, to marry, especially at such a young age."

"No mum, it's not your fault. Demetris was a wonderful person, we had good times together and we had two wonderful children, I can't deny all of that. Sometimes I feel I didn't do everything I could for him.

"Many nights I speak to him, I tell him about the children and I cry in regret. At other times I tell him that I did well, that I gave him everything I could, that we were happy. The crazy love, the enthusiasm, love alone doesn't always lead to happiness. Look at what's happening around us. I don't even know what would have happened if instead of Demetris, I had met and fallen in love with Dionysis at a younger age. I never went into the process of comparing. I think we should never compare two people that have played such an important role in our lives, that's being unfair to both of them.

"It's just that the timing I met Dionysis was perhaps the moment you were worried about for so many years, that at some point it would happen. It happened under tragic circumstances, as I said, and he rescued me and put himself forward, and broke his marriage. Now he has come back into my life and has knocked on my door, under very different circumstances, due to a book that the guy Yiannis Aidonidis wrote and I don't even know how all of this sticks together."

Paulina started crying and Pauline started talking. "Listen my love, you know me, I see things more rationally and not that tragically. It's obvious that this book you are referring to, as you say, is your story. Well I would be very happy if someone wrote a book about me."

They all laughed, the atmosphere lightened up and Pauline carried on talking.

"So, you have to go to Cyprus and find this Yiannis, whatever you call him. I can't imagine the shock he'll have when you tell him who you are. You'll find out more from him. And then you'll work out what is the best thing to do. Firstly, you have to get to know the facts."

"My dearest Paulina, even ignoring all this logic I still think, that you have to chase after your dream that is knocking on your door once more after all these years. It's like a comet that passes from the earth once again, after so many years and we are sitting here discussing about whether it's going to happen like this or like that and why and because…leave all this behind, close your eyes, believe and move on. See where it takes you."

Ms Orthodoxia nodded and approved of her friend's advice.

"Pauline has summed it all up. You need to have faith in things, let yourself be led, life is not a mathematical equation."

"It's strange," said Paulina, "you mentioned the comet that passes by the earth every so often and I have thought of the same thing. Could it literally be my star and after so many years of roaming around it has come to find me once again to lead me in the right direction?"

The three women continued talking, they drank their coffee, walked through Hyde Park, on the Kensington Palace side, and reached Bayswater where they had a delicious Chinese lunch at Queensway, a road in which no shop closes throughout the 365 days of the year.

When they finished their lunch, they were offered Chinese Fortune cookies with old riddles, proverbs and supposedly one's future. Paulina's said: 'Happiness is to love someone, to do what you love in life and have something to hope for'.

The Author and his Heroine

The beautiful hotel at the entrance to Limassol was packed with people. Posh cars rushed in and out and the guards of the hotel flew here and there to take care of the clients in their parking , the well dressed ladies with their coats and to help with information about the hotel. They did anything possible in this high peak time for everything to run smoothly. There were many people; VIPs, other guests, reporters, writers and others who were there for the event.

Yiannis had arrived that morning with his parents and they had lunch at the big diner of the hotel with the sea as a backdrop. He wanted to bring his parents along, and they also wanted to come, they wanted to spend time with him for the few days that he would be on the island; his parents were happy to have him there, even if only for a short while. At lunchtime, things nearly took a bad turn when the conversation turned to Alkis.

"Why didn't Alkis want to come with you?" asked his mother. "Is he ill? The other day, when I spoke to him, he didn't seem himself."

"He's fine mum, don't worry, he knows how to look after himself."

But his father added:

"Yes, but it's time for him to come home also, to start his life, get married, have a family."

"Are you set on getting us married dad? I've told you before; when the time comes you'll be the first to know. Alkis is well where he is. Leave him alone, he knows what he's doing, he likes Athens. You know how much he loves you, we both do. But he will make his decisions on his own. Look at me, I persisted and I didn't do that bad, did I?

"Anyway, let me tell you my news. I was going to come with my girlfriend, Erato. You've heard her name so many times; I think it's time for you to meet her. The rest you know, about her brother's death. What you don't know is that I was planning on asking her to marry me when we were here, at a special place I keep in my heart. It's been so long since we've been together. What do you say dad? And you mum?"

Both of their faces lit up, his mother got up and hugged him. His father, satisfied and proud of his child, also because he had asked him for his advice and approval indirectly as well as for his blessing, said: "You have my blessing son, do what you think is right. The reason we ask about Alkis is because we care. You both are our lives."

"I know dad, but I've told mum before. Don't pressure him. Leave him, he's well, there are homes with larger problems and we're trying to create some where there aren't any. I suggest we have our coffee and then go and rest for a while, the cocktail party later on may tire you out a little."

"What are you talking about?" his mother complained.

"They are going to honour our child and the ceremony is supposed to tire us out? Don't take any notice of our babbling Yiannis. Today is your day and we will be here to boast about you... but tell me, are Alexandros and Chloe fictional or are they real people?"

Yiannis lost it.

"You mean you've read the book?" and his eyes watered, taken by surprise.

"I read it and re-read it, me *and* your father. What, you think we wouldn't have read our child's book? Here, I have a copy in my bag that I want you to sign for us, we want to be the first to get a signed copy, before all your fans tonight..."

...in the big dining area in the centre of the room, Yiannis was sitting and signing books and exchanged amiable comments with different guests; a little while before they had prefaced him with a special reference to his most recent book which was also the reason for today's cocktail party. Yiannis, grounded as ever, accepted all these comments humbly, with a conscience of measure; he didn't like big talk.

He continued signing books, speaking and thinking at the same time. His eyes turned to his parents who were standing to one side, proud of what they were seeing. They themselves didn't believe in what he was looking for, for so many years. On the other hand, they had brought him up, which means that unconsciously they had pushed him on this track, a road they had never dared to take themselves.

Yiannis looked up at the sympathetic but cold faces, fake ones, genuine ones, every type of person. He thought that he had succeeded, that finally everything he had believed in took flesh and bone. 'That's how it is; you have to fight for it, to mingle with your loneliness a lot, to keep on trying until you get justice. You mustn't put your mind to people who don't give you anything throughout your course. That's how people are. They don't really like difficult things, they can't take a position in these cases and they choose easy paths, the logical thing to do. That's what they have learnt to do, lest you feel bitter about those who don't take a position. On the contrary, this should make you more stubborn.

'But who is that lady? I have been looking at her for a long time now, standing there waiting for me. If she wants something why doesn't she come to me?'

At that point, it was as though she had read his thoughts and the lady with the beautiful and warm face moved towards him.

She offered her hand and said: "I'm Chloe."

In the beginning Yiannis didn't understand and looked at her in doubt but, when she repeated her name with certainty, Yiannis got up and, flushed, said: "I had a secret hope that this would happen one day. Welcome, Chloe."

"My real name is Paulina, you probably already know that, and the beauty of it is that I am working for the advertising agency that will promote your book in England and who organised this event in your honour. You haven't met me before because I live and work for the company in London and I only arrived in Cyprus last night. Anyhow, I wanted you to meet me as Chloe first, seeing as you have written about me, and then meet me with my professional identity since we'll be working together for a while. That's also the reason I read your book and, if I judge from what I've read, I must have a very good, sensitive person standing in front of me, a person who can understand the human soul.

"I've been watching you for some time now. It's a tough thing to do, watch a person who has written about you with such preciseness, yet not know him at all. I waited for people to part a little and then speak to you. And seeing as we will work together I took the liberty of coming over and ask you out for a coffee."

They had coffee together, and then a second one. They got friendly very quickly and they also had dinner together the following night and talked about so many things. Yiannis told her the whole story about how he had met Dionysis on a warm, humid day in summer, a day that changed his life forever. The author and his heroine met the next day as well and the day after that because they also had to speak about work. Paulina now wanted to help him with all her powers, to promote this book that talked about her life, without anyone knowing.

How many times, in fiction movies, in James Bond adventures or even in treasure hunts, there's a secret, a code, a key, a magic word? And usually, two people hold an end of the thread. Each start off, very far from the other end and each other, unwinding the thread in order to reach the other end and find their other half in front of them and ultimately reveal the big secret.

This is also what happened here. Paulina didn't know about Yiannis and Yiannis who knew Paulina, didn't know where to find her. Dionysis, who respected his vow until the last moment, never revealed any names. No one knew. Only a stranger on a bench of a monastery, on a warm afternoon had heard his confession.

Paulina knew everything about Dionysis, his family, his surname, his childhood home, his close friends. Yiannis, who got to know about their story didn't know who Dionysis was. He never looked for him, it wasn't right, and besides, he had promised not to.

Now that fate had brought them together they both held a key in their hands that opened up a small box with the rest of the pieces of the puzzle. They either had to throw the keys in the sea and collaborate only professionally, or they had to shake the waters that had been stagnant for so long, a big dilemma. Sometimes in life we shouldn't chase after mirages. Some chapters end, wounds heal and close up, things become easier.

On the other hand, stars make their own cycle in the sky and when they meet again they remind us that nothing ends. When a concatenation of events, coincidences and incidents, can nullify all rules of statistics and possibilities, you ask yourself why!!!

Paulina had made her decision, on a wet morning a couple of weeks beforehand in Finchley, and confirmed it when she met with her mother and Pauline. Her meeting with fate wouldn't go by unattended. That's how the first key was discovered. She told Yiannis, Dionysis's name, who he was, where he lived, his childhood address that is, and people who could help him find him.

Yiannis had to take all this information in order to find Dionysis. Yiannis was known but he was also a stranger. Now in the sense that his articles were recognised in newspapers with his name, his book was gradually getting to be heard by word of mouth and his photo was published in magazines, he was known. On the other hand he was a stranger because he could ask anything and anyone to find out whatever he wanted to know about Dionysis without being suspicious. This is what he did and he discovered a whole lot of things about his friend, who now lived in Thessaloniki.

His 'friend'. Could he really use this term, did he have the right to? Yes, the right was given to him by Dionysis, when one afternoon he told him his story. Who knows, Dionysis might have felt that, the moment he deposited his soul to a stranger, he could trust in this person.

The words 'friend' and 'friendship' have strange meanings. There are friends who come in contact once a year and friends who are inseparable and see each other on an everyday basis. A rare kind, as a song says. You are born with your relatives, but throughout your life, you choose your friends.

Most friendships are made in school, during the most innocent years of our life when your character is being formed. You make fewer during your studies or when you start working. And then of course you meet your spouse, and a common circle of friends is formed, some you like some you don't and sometimes a man or a woman can become your friend.

'But during your school years,' thought Yiannis, 'that's when the most work is done, for sure.' That's when you make friends with complete and utter innocent motives, before the syphilis of the soul, before economic interests come into the picture. Of course, often, as you grow up and start forming strong and whole opinions many friendships are tried. Two people can start moving in different directions. Their habits become different, their philosophy of life, their partners, the way they progress, the way they handle the system.

Is this really how things are though? How much does this logic deteriorate? Is the choice that you made when you were a teenager, when you completely accepted the other as he or she was, with his or her good and bad traits, not right? Everything is relative. But friendship, as is love, is perhaps something deeper. It is being able to get over your logical limits, to ignore them, and hurt for someone, to offer them everything unconditionally. As parents do for their children. Not to seek for explanations, not to look for something in return.

Yes, Yiannis saw Dionysis as his friend. The understanding, their chat, whatever they shared that afternoon stamped their friendship, whether they came in contact again or not.

Chloe and Alexandros

Yiannis acted like lightning and found out everything he wanted about Dionysis, his family, his life in Thessaloniki, his job, everything. He made his decision immediately. He booked a ticket and prepared to go and find him. Costas, the other missing link in this whole story also helped.

Paulina brought him and Costas in contact, who even he himself, after meeting Paulina the way he had, had started believing in dreams and the conspiracy of the universe, and gave everything to Yiannis, addresses and telephone numbers. He also took care not to tell Dionysis, whom he spoke to regularly on the phone, that, during that week, Yiannis would be in Thessaloniki.

Yiannis was sitting in his seat on the aeroplane that had just taken off for Thessaloniki. His job in Cyprus had gone well, although this wasn't of much importance anymore. He knew that from the moment he worked hard at things, things would go well. Anyhow, it didn't take him long to see this side of Paulina as well; a professional in her all. A quality she had developed immensely while she was in London. She had disciplined herself in a torturing fashion and obliged Yiannis, every time they met, to talk about work first, about the book and its promotion, about the translation and then about what concerned her, her life, and her wellbeing. They had come close, they spoke to each other comfortably, and she spoke a lot about what had happened some years ago.

He sat calmly and when he had finished his coffee that a young stewardess had offered to him, he asked for another one, and took the book out of his bag.

On the front cover was a blurry picture of the monastery. He admired it, he opened up the book, saw his name and felt his heart grow, his eyes water. He had made it, he had written his best book, and its recognition was knocking at the door, at home and abroad as well. And then he read the dedication he had written: '*To an anonymous friend of the Monastery of the Fools and to all of those who believe in dreams.*

Truly, we pick up a book, we open it and start cowardly travelling to other worlds for a couple of days and this book becomes our best friend for a while and, when the story finishes, we feel some kind of euphoria and faith and at the same time loneliness for having lost a friend who now will only exist on our small bookshelf, silently.

Yiannis had always loved books, they were really his friends and he felt lonely when he finished reading them. He loved them very much and, when nobody was around and he wasn't embarrassed, he would speak to them. He gave them flesh and bone with his imagination and talked to them. Sometimes he took the same book and read it again and discovered something else and this happened over and over again. He also placed them in a certain order on the shelves, and dusted them, and later, when he grew up and made his choices, he recollected them and wrote small phrases from the books he had read. He always had them well kept in his soul and his parents' house.

His books meant everything to him. And now he was holding his own, best book in his hands. Suddenly he felt an unbeatable wish to open up the book and fall on a page randomly. He started inhaling the words manically as though he was reading it for the first time, as though he himself had nothing to do with the story, as any reader would have.

"...their meetings were scarce and short. They used an apartment that Alexandros had and was not rented. They also met at the Monastery of the Fools. He had taken her there on one of their first dates and since then, they went there regularly and sat like two good old friends and talked to each other sitting on a bench by the monastery. And they didn't feel

bad, or guilty, they spoke about themselves with no implications, about their lives.

Chloe played a dangerous double game. She had, in any way possible, to trap him, without anyone she knew seeing them. When the vagrant asked her where the meeting was to take place, she would disorientate him. She didn't want to expose Alexandros entirely and she didn't know how far this vagrant and his friends would go.

Of course she wasn't stupid. She knew that behind all this lay other big interests, that this rogue in which she so naively believed, was just a pawn on the chessboard of financial interests. The more time went by and the more she got to know Alexandros, the more she wanted to see him, but she had to do this as little as possible, if she wanted to do what was good for him.

The pressure on the other hand was unbearable. They had now told her expressively that on a specific date she had to bring them some elements that would expose him. Otherwise...Her husband told her that he had started receiving phone calls which, once answered, hung up. The walls had started closing in on her. Alexandros was a gentleman, but also was her husband, a husband with whom she never fell in love, but who wasn't to blame, for her children, the scandal, her children above all. "My God, forgive me and help me," she would say over and over again and her soul trembled in front of the possibility that this whole story would be revealed.

The door opened. Alexandros was impatiently waiting for her and kissed her affectionately. He hid her in his embrace and she broke out in tears. Her watery eyes had taken a dark tone, a tone of love, a honey-like colour that all eyes in love have, a sign of mutual understanding. Sometimes words are unnecessary. Body language, movements, the eyes, and expressions, reveal the soul.

Alexandros looked at her and didn't avoid his glance. The game couldn't go on any more. This man wasn't, unfortunately for her, an arrogant, modest middle-aged businessman with a belly, a cigar and snobbery. He was a simple, good man, so good with her that she fell in love with him.

Each time they met they would get closer to each other, their talks were endless, they listened to each other talking about themselves, about their family, their dreams. The speechless wall clock would interrupt them, or the bells of the evening mass, telling them it was time for them to part. The anticipation, the telephone calls, the heartbeats, the butterflies in their stomachs before each encounter, created a teenage fever that scared them, and created guilt in both of them. The downhill, the abyss, Chloe's desperation after their last embrace, but mainly the erotic kiss and the goodbye, all were an indescribable loneliness.

"What's wrong my love?" He asked her. It was the first time he called her 'my love'. How tragic! It's during moments of crisis that everything comes to the surface. But that 'my love' he said, made her finally decide. Things were simple, they had to stop here, at any cost. She had made a mistake, but this was the limit, the consequences burdened her, she had no right to destroy another person to save herself, even though she wasn't sure she could save her own self.

Chloe was a good person. Suddenly her eyes took on an amazing severity that scared Alexandros. With the truth, righteousness consolidated in her mind with those two words 'my love', everything was clear.

"Sit down," she said, "I want to tell you a little story about me that will shake you and bring many small-scale explosions in our lives, but I believe that you have to know and from there on you will act accordingly..."

Chloe finished her narration. She told him everything from beginning to end. The relief she felt was huge, even though this also may have meant a lot of bad for her too. Sneers, condemnation from all sides, she may even lose her husband, as well as Alexandros whom she had been looking for all her life and whom she met under the most tragic circumstances.

She knew she was doing the right thing though, she always did but she didn't know how to find the courage to move on. Now she had found it and this, God helped her with. She may have been a whore in the body, maybe she had made tragic mistakes, but she would not humiliate her soul, ever. She carried on talking, words were coming out by themselves, creating a mirage.

She was looking for a response from Alexandros, some kind of sign, a question, a clarification perhaps, but nothing. He just listened with a harsh, dark look, not a bad one or in defiance, but tough. If Chloe had drawn some holy force and she had said everything so realistically and bluntly, the person that she now had in front of her was ten times stronger to a point that she was scared. But she couldn't go back now. His gaze was penetrating, tormenting, it was dictating her to carry on, and she did until she finished, she had nothing more to add.

She didn't even say sorry, she knew she was offending him. The couple of minutes that intervened were like those that seemed to last for an eternity. Literally, everything stopped; time, life, their heartbeats. Every now and then you could hear a drop of water dripping from a loose tap into the sink, you could hear a shed squeaking from the wind on the roof of the block of flats, you could hear the hands of the clock on the wall ticking, an insect outside on the balcony, the singing of a bird that was sitting on the branches of a tree which nearly touched the veranda of the small flat on the second floor of the building.

"I need all the information you have, phone numbers, descriptions and anything else about these people who are blackmailing you," said Alexandros breaking the silence. She mechanically gave them to him. He took them and got up decisively.

"Was anyone following you?" he asked her.

"I think not," she answered, "I made sure I always gave wrong information about our meetings and up until now I fooled them. I think no one knows this place or where I am now."

"Okay," he said decisively, "go home and forget everything. Give yourself fully to your family and everything will be all right. No one will bother you ever again. And look after yourself." He kissed her on the cheek and when she went to hug him he pushed her away softly.

He opened the door and told her to be as quick as she could. Chloe who was as white as a sheet, a relic, moved on slowly towards the stairs and only turned once to see him for the last time. He was standing at the door watching her rush off. He smiled at her sadly and that smile, that image, since then, she never forgot. She carried it with her like punishment, a wound that would remind her of what she did.

She went home and she had three choices. To collapse and reveal everything to her husband; to commit suicide, or to smile and give herself to her family even more and hope. To take her own path on her own and try and get over it. But to forget, how could she forget? At least live in the ruins of her soul and, who knows, maybe at some point hope would be born there, where everything had been burnt down by the flames of her sins and of the tragic situation and games that life had played on her.

Every person has to love themselves, to try and become better, to accept the rotten pieces on themselves and move on. And so Chloe chose the third road and hoped that the wounds would heal without no further or additional complications. And her prayers were heard...

Alexandros, as soon as her figure disappeared, stopped living. He closed the door and pushed it slowly with his back until he collapsed to the floor. He stayed there as though lightning had struck him, he didn't even know how long he stayed there for.

In the beginning he wasn't capable of thinking about anything, he remained there looking at the wall opposite him and the soulless objects spread around the flat. The objects, one by one started moving and prepared their own show. Not as tragic as the previous show that was revealed two hours beforehand. The performance that was playing on the wall opposite was the life of Alexandros. Of this simple, hardworking, bright and decisive man whose goodness bothered others and made them decide to destroy him.

He saw his childhood years pass in front of him, his school years, the army, his university years, his work, his relationship with his wife, his marriage, his personal progress and his children. Whatever he treasured most in his life was in danger of falling apart and he would have a huge responsibility for this. The performance was on the verge of ending. The chairs were moving, the mirror spoke, the clock on the wall was looking straight into his eyes, the lights turned on and off, the plates had set up a dance like an ancient tragedy, as though there was whole pandemonium going on and everyone was waiting for an exit, the big finale...he jumped up, all sweaty, while outside, nightfall had arrived. He had a lot to do. He first had to save Chloe and then himself.

Everything took place methodically and fast with extreme effectiveness. Alexandros found one of his close friends who worked in the department of crime prevention and gave him the telephone number and the details of the blackmailer. They had to bring him in for a different reason and attain information in exchange of his release.

They didn't find any kind of difficulty and soon enough the guy revealed everything. He revealed his collaborators and slowly the clue of Ariadne started unravelling itself and the facts pictured a huge competitive fight against Alexandros, another businessman, who had invested everything in an offer, which, it seems, would fail due to the winning of the contract by Alexandros's company.

Alexandros found him and made him see him under his terms. As usually happens in such cases, in the beginning, the other denied everything and then went into attack mode, but soon found out that he had a very good player in front of him with many aces up his sleeve. Alexandros, who was well prepared, told him that if he ruined his home and exposed the girl involved in this spider's web, he would take them all down. He offered him the job in exchange for destroying everything they had against the girl and he meant every word of it.

Even to frauds, words mean something. In some cases it may even be words that are stronger than anything else. This happens when they have someone in front of them who not only doesn't bluff, not only isn't scared, but has the morals to which they themselves bow to. The interests bowed in front of this person. The storm thrashed, the vagrant was surprised and never opened his mouth again because there was a lot against him that wasn't in his best interest to fight against, not even to remember what had happened.

A couple of years later they killed him in front of the court house. It was only a matter of time. He had disturbed someone else and, usually in such cases, justice is done in different ways, in primitive ways, with no indications, no worldliness, no legal procedures. It seems that he had abused an underage girl. Her mother killed him on the spot, outside the court house on the day of the trial. All he got was a couple of months in jail as a penalty and perhaps bail. And so the mother took the law into her own hands, destroying her own life on the way. Wrong, no one deserves something like this for a bastard, but surely many were happy. One of these people was Chloe.

The competitor accepted the job offer and gave a huge part of it to Alexandros's father-in-law's company. Alexandros went to his wife and told her the story, a little altered of course. He told her that they had hired a whore who was blackmailed into trapping him. That in the beginning he had fallen for it and had fallen into her tentacles. And that, even though he realised what was going on and he had already dealt with everything, he hadn't acted respectfully and he wanted a divorce. It was also perhaps, an opportunity, as he explained to his wife, for them to see their relationship more seriously, to stop pretending and hurting one another.

Things were not going well with his wife but he adored his children. Anyhow, he was always burdened by the fact that he worked for his father-in-law. The bad-mouthing, mainly in the beginning, they called him an adventurer. Regardless of the fact that during his course he had shown outstanding business ingenuity, he had provided for the company, he had brought it to an enviable level, he was correct and honest, he was very tired. Therefore he declined the advice even by his father in law to try and stay in his marriage and that everyone had girlfriends, but that the importance lay in treating your wife like a queen and he chose the difficult way out.

He wanted to be free at any cost; he wanted a divorce with any price. Everything well and holy, but no one could understand why he took everything so much to heart. Even his wife understood, after the first scenes and relevant actions to save her dignity, she realised that he wasn't bluffing but she couldn't imagine her life and her social life without Alexandros.

No one knew though, no one had understood why, except for a stranger, Alexandros was taking such harsh measures, because, for the first time in his life he had loved a human being so much. And he pushed this person away, this woman who could have ruined him because she wanted to escape from the parasites in which she had got into once and for all.

As for Chloe, she begged to God every day for nothing bad to happen. Every time she heard the phone ring she thought that this was it, everything was finished. Every time her husband walked into the house she expected him to jump at her and make a fool out of her in front of her children. Nothing like this happened though and gradually the nightmare subsided. Peace and calmness came to her soul and her home..."

Suddenly Yiannis found himself back to reality. He closed the book and looked outside the window. Greece's second biggest city was beautiful and it was getting closer and closer. Dionysis, hiding behind his anonymity and the masses for a few years now, was somewhere down there expecting him. He was expecting his friend Yiannis, he was expecting to introduce themselves to each other properly and have a cup of coffee together.

A New Life

Seeing as the storm hits you inexorably, it manages somehow, one hit after another, and suddenly silence comes. There when he thought that everything was lost, there when he was slapped in the face time after time, that he couldn't venture out of things, as though he was an outcast of society, suddenly everything subsided, small rays of sunlight started entering the dungeons of his soul and clearing out the bad.

Mr Aristides trusted him and didn't regret it. Dionysis soon showed his good character, he worked hard, with good judgment. With the first opportunity he became head engineer and started taking on bigger projects by himself. He started making much more money; he bought a second-hand but good car, a small Fiat that suited him fine.

The great thing was that not one of his colleagues ever doubted him. In the beginning there was distance and some mistrust that was understandable. Slowly though, they all realised that this man didn't have any hidden agenda. He was willing to help anyone who needed his help at work, he revealed all his knowledge and won them all over. And because he didn't give importance to scheming, intrigues and such things that you usually find in big companies, he was clean, everyone respected him. He was also outspoken. What he wanted to say or do, he did. He respected the team but also had his opinion.

When it was asked of him, he studied all the projects of the company in depth, the costs and its winnings. He made a couple of simple but very rewarding suggestions and the company started gaining power. He too got stronger along the way, especially inside. He started living again, spoke with his children, his father, he saved money and put some aside. He had two hoards, one for Costas who had helped him and one for his children.

Time went by and he started smiling again. He nonetheless was human too, with needs, and he started socialising, he went out with his colleagues and a couple of friends that he had made. One of these was Aristarchos whom he had met at Mount Athos and whom he gradually got close to. He had also helped him a lot.

When they went back to Thessaloniki, Aristarchos invited him to his home for dinner, where he met his family. Dionysis made him tell him everything about his job, his professional mistakes, the promises he had made to the banks that he couldn't keep. Things weren't that good, the debts were big, the financial side of things barely covered him.

Dionysis sat him down and obliged him to discipline himself. "The biggest problem," he said, "is to admit your mistakes and change the way you work which obviously wasn't succeeding." In the beginning Aristarchos came up with one excuse after another, you see he was closed up in his little box for years, he had learned to do things in a specific way and he didn't want to change. In time though he saw that what his friend was telling him had good results.

They went to the bank together and talked to his creditors and restructured all his obligations in a way that he could respond to and wouldn't constantly drown in him stress. Gradually the big change was happening and this was due, in a big part, to Dionysis. The two men built a close relationship and saw each other mend in different ways.

Dionysis's business mind and his experience, as well as the positive energy he let off, made him get into the financial side of the company instead of the technical department. Mr Aristides was intelligent and open-minded and it didn't take him long to realise that he could trust this young man and place him in financial matters and secrets of the company.

Dionysis, after his divorce, swore that one day he would build something completely of his own, he owed it to himself. At the same time though, he was a man dedicated to the people who employed him, to those who helped him. And he showed it. Up until now, none of his employers was ever scared of losing him or think that he would harm the company. On the other hand no one took him for granted because he was a man who inspired respect, he had this gift. It's difficult to explain sometimes, but some people bear a form of nobility, manliness, something aristocratic that everyone is excluded to.

When the company grew, along with its profits, when he finally made it, and this didn't happen in a day or two of course, he started studying strategic moves and this is when the issue of Albania came up. On a Saturday morning, Mr Aristides, as usual, regardless of his age, went on long walks and philosophised, loved his morning coffee, and invited him to his house to make him an offer. A couple of years had gone by and the two men had come close, there was a mutual trust.

"Look Dionysis, I've been in this business for fifty years now, and thank God, I've created a respectful fortune as well as a good company. As the young uneducated contractor that I was I managed to create a company with many employees and huge projects. I always asked about what I didn't know, I never pretended that I knew everything and I think that's why I did well. Now I have to do another clever thing. As you know I have three children and only the middle one, Stefanos, loves this job and is also good at it.

"Christna, my eldest one is a phychologist and she works as a social worker on a part time basis with retarded children. That's what she chose, that's what she loves. And my philosophy has always been to let my children do what they love, so that they can be good at it.

"The young one became an archaeologist and, as you know, she is here the one moment and there the next. Anyhow, she isn't married either. So, I want to do two things. First, I slowly want to pull out of the company and let Stefanos take over, and second, I want to bring other shareholders on board, so that the company can continue to exist and progress. Needless to say that at the same time i want to protect the rights of my other children as simple shareholders. I don't mind having fewer shares in a bigger company that I have founded. This of course has to happen carefully and safeguards and controls have to be put in place in order to avoid any disputes and fearful disagreements.

I have invited you here to ask you if you are interested in becoming a shareholder, but also to ask you your opinion about all this seeing as I believe that, besides an honest and direct person, you also know how to balance things well."

Dionysis told him his opinion, he asked for time in order to think about the offer and then, a few days later accepted it. He would take a small percentage and being insightful, he put down a condition that they would expand the company in the Balkans where there was a boom in reconstruction, mostly in Albania, a country that was prejudiced, a country that, for years was cut off from the rest of the world...

For some people they say that whatever they touch it becomes pure gold, that they carry a karma with them, and without there being any scientific explanation, they have rare virtues which when they surface, scare the person in question as well. In the past, success scared Dionysis, although he sought it. Maybe he wasn't ready for it, maybe because it was only synonymous with money. In Cyprus money counted a lot, but certainly in the course of his life he had realised that it's not a measure of happiness or success just by itself.

Now Dionysis was ready. He had a lot of supplies on his side, mainly all the blows he had had in the past. Nothing goes to waste if you use all the negative things that happen to you and turn them into positive.

The company got new shareholders, Mr Aristides started pulling out, Stefanos was capable and well -loved and took on the reins. Dionysis got into the administrative council and took on the Albania project.

He went to Albania many times, taking on the procedures of organising the company. He made slow and steady moves and when he felt strong enough, opened up a small office there, he bought some land in Tirrana and the company took on the construction and sale of buildings, offices and apartment blocks.

He was returning to Salonika from such a trip tonight sitting in a taxi which was taking him from the airport to his home. As he stared out the window he suddenly saw it. Completely naked, a gold disc, completely round in the clear December sky. The blistering cold crossed your bones and this image came to suddenly awaken a sweet memory. He looked up at the moon again and in its frame he saw Paulina's silhouette. His heart warmed up.

'I wonder where she is, what she's doing?'

The silhouette was there, intense, she was looking at him and was smiling and he felt the same touch as a few years back. Their first talk, their first kiss, the quilt, the heartbeats. He smiled. It was strange, he didn't feel any pain anymore but a sweet, melancholic feeling.

"Paulina," he whispered... "you see, slowly-slowly we made it."

"Yes, Dionysis, we made it. We survived and moved on, thank the Lord."

He was certain about this answer.

The Flame that Never Burnt Out

...they met in a small wood behind the monastery. Everything around them had become paralysed. It was like a huge invisible veil was covering the woods in order to protect them and the feeling that they were entirely by themselves had created sentimentalism, a plethora of emotions, peace, as well as making their hair stand up all over their bodies. The butterflies left their stomachs and went up into the skies enjoying the light of life. His heart was also beating wildly and arithmetically, as though his whole life was marching in front of him, everything he had done, everything he hadn't done but wished he had, all his musts and all his don'ts...

They approached each other and held hands while their faces came very close to each other. A tiny distance was the only thing that separated them; they felt each other's breath. Such a small distance that allowed but a small ray of light from the moon to pass in between them, naked in the open sky. Dusk was subsiding and night was falling and was taking the sceptres from the golden disc of the sun which was setting.

Oh the moon, their companion on so many nights when they were whispering messages to each other and sent conceivably via the moon to their recipient. And the moon, which knew so many secrets, which saw everything, a missing link, because it could see both of them, at the same time, and they knew this and used the moon as their messenger.

Their lips united in a cool kiss, a soft velvety touch. The touch strengthened, the kiss became passion and then suddenly they pulled back from each other as though an electric shock had hit them. It was something more, it was just the realisation of the immensity of what they were living.

Primitive feelings, feelings that touched their every cell, feelings that upset their inner selves and also cleared them from all the bad feelings they had kept inside. He opened up her shirt and continued looking at her, while his eyes shone strangely in the moonlight.

They kissed again passionately each trying to penetrate one into the self of the other. They sat on the humid ground that was covered by a carpet of wild grass with the leaves of autumn. They had never united, they were always careful of what they did, one held back the one time, one held back the other. Now they were not controlling anything though, their bodies were shaking, their souls were in complete harmony.

They rolled in the earth and he found himself on top of her seeking her breasts. She let him, she led him to her aroused nipples that leaked love and he sucked at them with greed. Paulina's moans along with his shortness of breath empowered and completed the scene.

He lifted up her skirt, while she undid the zip of his trousers. He embraced her with his clothes still on and both started to move in rhythmical motions at the rhythm of their groans. Gradually the pressure on her grew and suddenly the clothes disappeared and he entered her with passion, while she let out a loud cry. They united their lips and rolled like crazy on the ground.

Their orgasm was simultaneous, their release from their bonds had come like a storm that came and left. Paulina started to cry and he kissed her on her wet eyes. They hugged tightly and kissed. The conclusion of their story had been written. Two people with rich internal worlds, two people who were looking to save their soul, two people who were alone were united forever...

...he opened his eyes abruptly, looked around him and for a couple of seconds he was lost. The taste of the kiss was still fresh on his lips, a sweet soft taste, a numbness of the whole body, a trip from beyond, back to reality, while he started to recognise the furniture and the different objects in his room. He looked high up on the ceiling, like a big screen at the movies and he saw, with dizzy speed and, in repeat, the dream from which he had just awoken.

He and Paulina were wrapped in a cloud that covered the Monastery of the Fools and the area around it, they were in each other's arms having become one after the one and only contact that they never had. But alas this was a dream, that had been coming and going for so many years now, first in the small flat that he had rented when he first arrived in Thessaloniki, afterwards in the other bigger place and now in the luxurious, private, three-bedroom flat of the construction block of the company. As he was there lying down looking at the ceiling he thought that, if he turned to the right, he would feel Paulina's warm velvety body. He felt her fragrance all over his body. What was this again?

He got up, he switched the coffee machine on, put a nice music disc on and went to the bathroom for a quick shower. Then he shaved, got dressed quickly and sat in front of the bay windows to have his coffee, to meditate, plan his day, have his cigarette and head off to his office. This is what he did nearly every day. He liked this routine, he liked enjoying small joys in life. And so the first coffee of the morning and the planning of the day at home was a habit he never changed. Without anyone bothering him, with no telephones ringing, a couple of minutes of self-concentration in order to charge his batteries for the rest of the day.

A little while later he would come out, elegant, as always, but not overly dressed, from the entrance of his apartment block. He would exchange a couple of words with the guard, and along with the wonderful tormenting taste of Paulina's kiss still in his mouth he would head to the office. A ten-minute walk in the cold, but on this sunny day in December, it was ideal.

At the same time, someone else, a couple of blocks away, did approximately the same things in his hotel room. A warm shower, a shave and breakfast in the dining room of the hotel. Yiannis ate lightly and on the spot, after he had kindly smiled at the comments of the oldish employee of the hotel who had recognised him and stated that she was a fan, he ordered a coffee and started drinking it slowly as he lit a cigarette.

Approximately six years had passed and in a while he was going to meet the man he had met one afternoon at the monastery and had had the most honest and essential chat that he had ever had with anybody, especially a stranger. Was their encounter a coincidence or was it what we call fate, destiny?

In the end everything happens for a reason. His decision to divert towards the monastery, the story he heard, his brave decision to leave for Greece, 'therefore' he thought, 'our course in life has already been decided.' 'Not exactly, he answered himself, 'there are signs, there are opportunities, but it also depends a lot on the choices we make.'

He finished his coffee and his cigarette, he got up, went into his room, pampered up a little, took his scarf and his overcoat and decisively walked out. He had found out the location of the offices of the company where Dionysis worked. Thank God for Paulina and Costas of course who had given him very instructive information. On the previous night, when he had gone to the hotel in a taxi and settled in, even though it was really cold outside he took a walk to realise where he was, to know exactly where to go the next day and he knew that it would take him around ten minutes to get to his final destination.

Parallel Lives

Thoughts, thoughts, thousands of thoughts. The mind travels, it imagines, it dreams, it builds. The thought is free, its speed is faster than anything else. Maybe the speed of light might prove us wrong. The speed of light that transforms everything into energy, that helps us travel in time, back and forth. But can thoughts also go back in time? Thoughts can go around the world not in eighty days but in eighty minutes. They make you a hero, a princess, a supporter of the poor and the weak. At times they perk you up, at others they limit you, they whip you. Personal problems, professional ones, bad situations, dead ends, start of a tempest in the mind. Some think sickly, others morally, one has a clear conscious, and the other has everything confused inside his head.

Yiannis and Dionysis had the same way of thinking and they realised this from the first moment they spoke to each other, that's why they trusted one another. This way of thinking didn't belong to many, neither was it a way of thinking of the herd, of the easy way out, the accommodating one. Their thoughts had to do with substance. For them, the truth, what is wrong and right, what is legal and illegal wasn't found in the grey zones. The above meanings ran through the rivers of their souls, like limpid waters that watered their every cell.

When Dionysis went to Mount Athos he found out that they called this something else. They called it 'Virgin Mary's Orchard'. Yes, truly, having stayed there for three days, he felt that he was in a huge orchard full of flowers, beautiful flowers everywhere. And the one flower complemented the other and fragranced, all of them together, beautiful fragrances, sweet ones that soothed the pain that healed the soul.

After coming back from Mount Athos, back to the reality of the big city, he felt as though he was out of his league. He went back to his routine, his daily life, in the struggle for survival.

As he moved along he remembered the words of Father Vonifatios, when he said that monastic life and predominantly the life of the one practising it, is like climbing up a rigid mountain, while in a cosmic life, everyone lives according to their decisions and gets up his calvary that is more negotiable. He had thus, thought that things may not really be like this.

Society, the world, is also an orchard full of nettles and to be a flower in the middle of all these nettles is perhaps much harder than being a flower amongst many flowers, even if that is a harder world. It may be arrogant of him to call himself a flower in between nettles. On what criteria, with what facts, with what right? Honestly.

Dionysis was anything but arrogant. But he stood out, he was different from many people and he had this conscience, because he believed in righteousness, in truth, he had morals, he thought about his fellow man, he was respected. He receded in order to avoid misunderstandings, he always saw things from the other person's point of view as well, he wanted the good for the whole, he believed in equality, in freedom, in democracy.

And he put all these morals into practice, he experienced them, that's why he took difficult paths, and lonely ones, during which, on many occasions he got knocked down with the story that led to his divorce at the peak. He went aside from his children, and looked for another life. His own 'Virgin Mary's orchard'...

These thoughts were troubling him for a while, until a priest, that he had met in Thessaloniki and to whom he spoke now and then, told him two things clearly which satisfied this worry. First, that this 'Virgin Mary's Orchard', Mount Athos, is not only strewn with flowers, but it also has nettles, many weeds and parasites, maybe in a parabolic sense referring to bad moments, to miscalculations. At the same time he said that in 'Virgin Marys Orchard', the fight with the devil takes place chest to chest, it's tougher, wilder, and more inexorable. Like the war, when the enemy moves on to kill the officers and then the simple soldiers.

The second thing that he told him was an ancient Chinese but also Greek proverb that satisfied Dionysis then, very much. This utterance would say that the most beautiful flowers in the world, sprout, grow, become beautiful and smell between nettles...

Yiannis also walked ahead thinking of a load of things. Ten minutes can be enough to assess your whole life. When he finished his studies he had three choices. To stay abroad and make a career there, in a country in Europe, in England perhaps where he had studied or even in America, and why not in Canada. Second choice was to return to Cyprus and integrate himself as fast as he could into the system. That was what his parents wished for, a good job in the government, in a bank or in a semi-governmental organisation with good working hours, security and perhaps a second job, some private lessons for an extra income while letting life go by.

The third and most difficult one was to return to Cyprus and make his own choices!!! Not to accept the package deal that they had offered him, but take the best of the country(there were a lot of things he liked), as he identified via his own criteria. Other things, most things that were created by the system itself, to ignore and to corn

What naivety, my God, what an illusion! He returned to Cyprus and fought as hard as he could and, in the end, after many downfalls, few opportunities and wise thinking, he left and returned to his first solution and settled in Greece.

Both of them moved on in the cold winter, but on a sunny morning in December with quick steps, and they thought to themselves. Thousands of thoughts, thousands of images, a mosaic of images, people, incidents of the town, which woke up, slowly, and that started to breathe. The breaths multiplied, steamed, warmed up the air as the city awoke, got warmer, and prepared its own concert for the day that rose. Thousands of instruments and voices composed sounds, pastimes, discussions, loves, fights, hugs, kisses. The birds, the trees, the cars, the horns, the buses, all these people, alive and soulless, participated in the symphony of another day of life...

Thoughts were silent, by the thousands they came and went in and out of Yiannis's and Dionysis's heads and they made a dialogue with these thoughts. They went into labyrinths and labyrinthine galleries and every thought brought another and the mosaic was building itself and had nothing to envy from the wonderful big mosaics that we usually see in museums and archaeological sites.

Yes, Cyprus was so beautiful, its cities, its villages, simple people, the hospitality, the pride, the neighbours, the family, the solidarity. Of course a word brings out positive vibrations, but the same word can, unfortunately, also bring negative ones.

Things had changed, especially after the coup d'état and the invasion. With the unbelievable destruction as an alibi, the eviction, the refugees, the civilian juxtapositions, came the indolence and love for the precarious. Many people who had built their lives lost everything in just a day. You need a couple of years to build your home; it took only one day to destroy it.

In the fight for survival started the objective for easy money, the precarious solutions. The hastiness and corruption started, the public services started to become very crowded with inefficient people who simultaneously engaged in second jobs. And then money came in from abroad, a lot of money in aid, tourism increased, the standard of living rose. At the altar of progress everything was sacrificed. The shaking of the hand, the honest agreements, the simple say of a man, all these things stopped existing and were replaced by lies and complicated, legal agreements. All the altars of money, materialism, glory, power.

Was there any progress? Of course there was, a lot of things changed for the better, the cities grew and got more beautiful, not without a price of course, the first victims being the souls of people which had frozen…and on the other hand, the" Cyprus Problem", always there like a big brother watching generations and generations of Cypriots being born and brought up and this problem remained unsolved, strong, an impossible bond, the ancestral sin. And on top of this whole problem, for which they(political parties and politicians) realised different opinions, which almost always ended in attachments to the past and accusations to each other, institutions were built, careers, political parties, politicians climbed up the ladders, which at times made you wonder what would happen to all these people if there were ever a solution. How right you are my poet from Alexandria when you were waiting for the barbarians…

«because it's dark and the barbarians have yet to arrive
And some have arrived from the borders
And they said that barbarians there are no more
And now what will we become without them
Those people were a kind of solution»

That's what happened and is happening in Cyprus. Then the drugs came, hooliganism, events of deeper social problems that brought a lot of prosperity, anarchy, impunity, intertwining, and lack of vision. And all this in a country of seven hundred thousand inhabitants, a country with educated people, where corruptness, though, is even more dangerous than in some third world countries, because it's invisible, it moves amongst people like vipers and it spreads its poison left and right. In the name of financial interests, for glory, for power. Friends of him used to tell him 'what's the point in analysing all this, are you going to change the world? These things happen all over the world.'

Yiannis tried to acclimatise to all this. He started accepting some things and not others. He became wiser, he became a silent observer. Along the way he realised that there were many observers like him, guards of hope, guards of the good and of righteousness, which on many occasions the law and the establishment didn't attribute to or when it did it was too late. But sometimes God intervened and restored the right. Holy Divine Justice was the hope that human smallness could not touch.

He didn't change the world, but he succeeded and continued to fight from a better and more powerful position and he also moved a pebble with his sweat, his worries and the hard work into the improvement of the social whole, of humanity, towards love and solidarity towards our fellowmen. And the sweat he poured didn't go to waste, because along with the labour of other lonely, anonymous people, even of graphic people, they also managed to water the orchard of life and contributed to sprouting flowers that perhaps one day would bring spring around.

Yes, Dionysis and Yiannis loved their homeland and, even though on many occasions they saw the glass half empty instead of half full, it was because they felt that their Cyprus and its people deserved better leaders, better lives, better solutions. Unfortunately though, many of the above were created by people themselves, an endless nefarious circle that wasn't easy to correct.

They would go to Dionysis and tell him: "You must hire this person, he is a good guy, he's the son of so and so." And he would answer: "If he's good at his job I will hire him, if he isn't, I very well might do him harm because it means that he is not suitable for the job in question," and he would change the conversation by disarming them.

He had his own rules, the rules he had been taught from his father, that he had himself shaped throughout his studies, his travels, his experiences and he followed these.

And like Christ, who taught such wonderful things that are still valid today for all civilisations and all peoples and he had to sacrifice himself to convince, give substance and credibility to everything he preached by his example and he was put up onto the cross into a Calvary and they crossed him, the same way Dionysis at some point, when it was needed, he did the right thing and left.

Yiannis also, when he realised that the frequency of his dreams was different from the ones of his beloved homeland, which he returned to with so many dreams before they were shattered by the rendering cogwheels of the establishment's machines, he left and looked for his luck elsewhere. And each managed, in the end, to become a beautiful flower in an orchard of nettles.

They continued walking in the noisy streets of the city while at the same time thought and looked around , like sleepwalkers of the performance going on around them. And when from time to time they would reach a crossing or traffic lights where they had to concentrate, return to the present, activating their instinct of survival, only then did both of them realise that all the time while they were walking and thinking, they made movements and looked around mechanically.

Thousands of thoughts crossed their minds and even so, during those three or four minutes they could not recall anything that happened around them. Apart from some images that had imprinted themselves in their memory and drifted and again like an addiction to the game of thoughts, where thousands of kaleidoscopes open up in front of them only for a couple of seconds or even some humongous long minutes in substance.

Such an image came and zoomed in Yiannis's photographic memory and threw him back in thought. The image of a small shop with a very old sign outside which said 'Shoe Repairs'. An old man was sitting inside his shop, a small room with a space not even two by three square metres , surrounded by thousands of shoes: men's, women's, high heeled, flat, with laces, without, summer shoes, winter shoes. Tools, sewing pins, tacks, varnishes, clothes for polishing, all served the art of this man that was sitting there hunch backed working with such care, with such yearning like a mother who was feeding her child with so much dedication.

'His children,' Yiannis thought, 'are the shoes.' He might have been doing this job for fifty, sixty years now and he loves and respects it. He comes in the morning, works, fixes, pieces up, shines and gets paid. Nothing complicated, like what most of us do. He doesn't owe anything to anybody and no one owes him anything. He works, gets paid in cash and with what he makes he gets by.

His mind ran to his friend, the varnisher in Athens who shined his shoes once a week and got the opportunity to have a chat. Truly, how many people lead a more simple life, how many people stand and enjoy the noises, the images, the smells, the taste of coffee, of food, touch life with care, with respect, like a precious object in the hands of a collector without wanting to conquer everything?

How many anonymous people are happier, more at ease with their peaceful life and us passers-by, who continuously run to anticipate the mirage that escapes us, we overtake these people, we don't turn to look at them, because what we have to do is so much more important that in the end the most important things escape us. The oxygen of life, a smile, its meaning...

Dionysis moved on also and thought to himself. He saw somewhere in the sky the night moon, and slight disc that disappeared with the light of day and recalled its night magnificence and his whispers to Paulina. He read somewhere, that in Korea the moon is the symbol of the family. Someone else told him that the moon represents completion, and perhaps the second version satisfied him more. It starts off like a small arrow in the sky and slowly-slowly it fills up, it fills up until completed. And then back to the start again. 'It seems like it's a celestial computer of human messages and thoughts,' Dionysis smiled.

As soon as a new moon commences, people start sending messages to each other via a bright screen until it's full. The most faithful to the partisans are the people in love. They exchange glances and messages and the computer fills up just like the big disc of the moon until it's a full moon, the emblem of completion.

And every full moon creates many families, couples, friends, associates and other beautiful relationships. Then someone comes along and empties the computer to give the opportunity to others to live their own maturation, their own full moon...

'What nonsense I think about,' Dionysis said, nearly out loud. 'I took the moon and made up my own story. Thank God I think of these things by myself because if anyone was to hear me, they would think I'm crazy.'

His conscience returned and slapped him.

'Don't underestimate yourself,' it said to him. 'Yes, if needed you need to become crazy, for you to stand out and move on in life, do as you wish to. Not only with the power of logic, but also with emotions and intuitions of the unreal. That of which we the very few only see. That of which showed you your own moon last night so big, so real, so perfect and complete. A bright frame which in the middle you could imagine the real portrait of Paulina...'

Two people stand at a distance of only a couple of steps from each other. Like two cowboys in the Far West who recount with their eyes and try to psychoanalyse one another but also to try and distract one another, to make them hesitate before the deadly pull of the trigger. Here no one is going to kill anyone. On the contrary, the confrontation has to do with the weighing of life of two people who are friends and who have only met once in the past.

In front of them the door of Dionysis's company's offices opens up at the entrance of the office majestically, where an aged guard in a uniform is ready to give the sign, not for battle but for the reunion. The eyes of one fixed on the other, everything around them frozen and still.

The cold air caresses their blushed faces, the sounds of the city compose an orchestra of a thousand instruments that are preparing to close up a chapter that started six and something years ago. And the people walking up and down suddenly become the audience at a performance that ends with an extended round of applause. Before the curtain closes, the two protagonists move forward one in front of the other, they stand at a breath's distance, they hold hands and on the spot they embrace each other tightly.

"I knew you would come," said Dionysis first.

"I was waiting for the right time and anyway I also had to bring you this," Yiannis said opening his briefcase and taking a book from it, their book. "It's the first copy," he continued "and it belongs to you."

"Thank you, but I have bought at least twenty copies so far and I am giving them as gifts to friends and people I know. Apart from those which I have kept for myself, of course. And I have read it so many times, and every time I discover something else about you, about Paulina, even about me..."

"But, come on, let's go, we have so much to tell each other. I want to buy you coffee, smoke a cigarette together and talk. Isn't that what friends do?"

Yiannis's eyes watered. That's what he had dreamt of too. He was a little bit nervous because he had written about the life of somebody without his permission. Under cover of course, but nevertheless it didn't stop it from concerning him.

Dionysis, however, seemed to have been giving more importance to the fact that they had met once more, nothing else. After so many years, he was just confirming what kind of person and how good a paste of a human Yiannis was. When we form an opinion about someone and we come out correct, it's a beautiful feeling.

"What do you mean a coffee, of course you wanted to say many coffees, and not just today," added Yiannis unleashing the sentimental climate.

"I have been dreaming about this moment for many years and I won't let it realise itself with just the one coffee."

Dionysis felt as if he was listening to himself speak, praising God and his good judgment, that he chose and succeeded to hit the bull's eye and met such a good person to open up to at a time of weakness or humiliation.

The curtain was drawn and the two protagonists embraced spontaneously once more, while their eyes and faces shined with happiness . That embrace marked the beginning of a beautiful and unselfish friendship that was born in a monastery, it grew and matured with a lot of loneliness as well as patience and was glorified with a wonderful book.

That tight embrace locked inside it some of the most beautiful things in the world, along with two names, Dionysis and Yiannis…

PART FIVE

Yiannis Aidonidis – The Author

When Yiannis was young he worshipped books. He would get lost in their stories and content, he read and re-read them over and over again and he would, himself, become their hero and made up his own stories with his fantasy in which he was the main character. Sometimes he would be Yiannis Ayiannis, sometimes the Count of Monte Cristo, sometimes d'Artagnan. At a later stage, he got to know another author, Cronin, and started reading books for older children and before he moved to reading books for more mature reading, he went through the Dreyfus case. He grew up, went to study and he started finding out about the magic of the Greek language and of Greek authors and poets.

He fell in love with the 'two Ks' as he called them, Kavafis and Kariotakis and then he also added the third K in the group – Karagatsis. Of course, after that the fourth K came along, not a Greek one this time, with Kundera and then a fifth with, Coelho(written with k in Greek). The Ks were a point of reference, as was the Z of Zorro, only this time, in literature. And he also loved many others, Samaraki and Marquez and later a compatriot, Omiros Avraamides. He read and read continuously and I mention the above people because not only did he read them but he also studied them. Many of their books marked him deeply and some he read over again. When he was a child he had learnt '*Les Miserables*' inside out and loved the heroes of the story and, when he grew up he loved authors, who made up his own heroes.

He had decided to study English literature and up until then, everything was going well. Usually that's what happens. The first twenty years of Cypriots are engraved, predetermined, not to say anymore. You are born, you grow up, you go to school, the army, you serve your homeland and then immediately after that you go for your studies or work. In the government, in a bank, there where everyone wants to accommodate themselves. He thankfully had escaped the 'curse', that of his father having his own business. My God, how tragic, at the age of twenty, there when you really don't know what you want in life, you're not able to have your own personal opinion.

'You have to study architecture; the offices are built already for you, you will take over the business, the name, the family business' the usual talk.

You may say that sometimes having many choices can be confusing, they paralyse you, they lead you to dead ends. Yes, but still, you are making decisions about your life, about your own happiness or your declinations. The same goes for marriage. Who thought, that on the day they get married, they will live with that person for the next fifty years of their life, at least. Unless they divorce or death parts them before.

And so they study what fate set out for them at the altar, to continue the name and the family business, and God forbid, but in many cases this business, in the second or third generation collapses. The vision that a grandfather had once started doesn't exist anymore, justified or not, because of mediocrity or of a power struggle between the children or grandchildren to have their own way.

You see companies with a history of a century collapse, they totter. Unless at some point, something happens, somebody is born along the way; in the genealogy tree, a branch which, led by its soul, carries a 'microbe' with it, the seed, the love for the object and revives the marginalised name and the vision of the great-grandfather.

Yiannis avoided all of this, but he found worse complications in front of him at a later stage. The road he had chosen to follow reminds one of those electronic games that children and adults play fanatically. When you get over an obstacle, the degree of difficulty increases, the passages become narrower, the sirens are more seductive, the complications are narrower, from 'Scylla to Charybdis'.

First it was the pressure of studying a profession that would bring money, a good position, prestige, then the patience to come back to Cyprus and accommodate himself somewhere, then it was the pressure of getting a governmental, public job. He had nearly surrendered and his last defences had nearly disappeared altogether.

He was educated, unemployed, and insecure in a small society chasing windmills. It was neither the right place nor the right time for chivalry. In a small society with a lot of complications and politics, with an ennobling corruptness, a lot of intertwining and savagery, it was very difficult to be asked what job he was doing and reply 'an author'. And to be a devil's advocate, this is so in many societies, even in the most progressive ones.

'And what have you written?'

'Nothing yet', or: 'a small collection of poetry,' of which no one has heard. He chose journalism to earn a living, to have a job, to do something he liked and keep the flame that was burning, faintly now, in the candle of his dreams. A lonely candle, forgotten in a candelabrum of an abandoned temple that was trying to keep a warm hope in the heart of people in a consuming society where success was synonymous with money.

Then, when the candle was about to burn out, two things happened that convinced Yiannis to follow his dedication to his Calvary. After the Calvary comes the resurrection. In order to attain something, to succeed in what you want, you have to believe in it yourself, you have to work hard. If you are different, you have to accept your loneliness and, as many times as you may fall down, you have to get up again and look out towards your star that will lead you to the Bethlehem of your dreams.

One of the many books that Yiannis read was '*Jonathan Livingston Seagull*'. One afternoon he had visited his friend the priest with whom they had attended the same school, and was three years older than he was. He had become spiritual and Yiannis confessed to him. He went to see him and, in their many conversations, then when they were countering his dead ends and choices, his friend told him to read that book and stop pressuring himself, to let things be dealt with by God a little.

Something tough to do because you never know when you're overdoing it or when you're doing nothing about it. A Greek proverb says: 'So Athena can help you, you must also use your hands' (God can only help you if you take action too). And when he tells you, let God act, you wonder where you have to set the limit.

"Do your job piously like Zorba the Greek," his friend the priest told him. "Don't look back, nor left or right, as you move along because you will fall. Look ahead and follow the road you have engraved always under the condition that you know exactly what you want. Work and learn and be patient and the opportunity will come, but you must believe as well, you have to let the initiative be God's and believe in his omnipotence.!

And so he read 'Seagull Jonathan' and found his first sign. He photocopied the page and always carried it with him. A paragraph from that book helped him see things differently, it empowered the flame, the candle lit up once more, the flame reached out to Yiannis's heart and was transmitted everywhere, like the 'Christ is risen' of the orthodox, in him, in his soul, in his body.

He remembered the heroes of his novels again and his favourite authors. And he understood one thing. If you want diligence, you have to stop loving money, if you want to learn at university, you have to stop thinking about grades, if you want to love, you have to stop thinking that you may be hurt; and not set terms. If you want to succeed, you mustn't think of failure, but about how you can become better after each fall, until you reach your final destination.

The second thing that happened was when he met Dionysis and listened to his confession. A confession from which Yiannis held onto and started creating. And for the first time, this unimportant journalist started writing as he felt.

Without trying to pretend to be the 'five Ks', or any other author he worshipped and loved. He started writing about what overflowed in him, his pen started to move by the flame in his soul, many times he even surprised himself with what he wrote.

He didn't try hard anymore, he just wrote, he didn't look for nice expressions but he wrote spontaneously, he wrote down his ideas. He wrote what he believed in, not what would sell, the one moment he wrote about coincidences, about crazy scenarios, about one process and the other, through stories of everyday life, he spoke about people and their internal world, about their limits, about love, about God, about happiness, about death.

And after all this the novel "*Witnessed by God and the moon*" was born, in which he wrote the story of Dionysis and Paulina and, indirectly his own. Not like a love story with complicated scenarios and a favourable ending, but more like a story of the people next door. Detecting their life, looking for the why's about each of them, creating his own heroes just like he was representing the whole of society. Stress, daily life, routine, the big questions that drift people into maelstroms.

The man of consumption who, like a puppet, is pestered in an electronic game trying to find the meaning of life and drifts into labyrinths and dead ends and returns like a wild beast in the roads that open up for him with the illusion that he is recognised and protected. Then satiated he asks for more and goes even deeper into his dead ends, to attain whatever he wishes for and then suddenly he discovers that he has become a slave of time and he can't anticipate to enjoy what he has fought for.

The slave of materialistic goods that thinks that hard work is equal to many hours of work, and that entirely ignores that hard work can just be done by practising the mind and body, and the harmony of all his energies that bring mental calmness along with it.

Yiannis loved wine. From a young age he drank house red wine that his grandfather made in the village, and later when he grew up he started studying, choosing, closing his eyes, smelling and tasting the wine and what it represented. The vines, his village, the grapes, Christ, the nectar, the deity Dionysus, the labour of farmers, a universal language, like music that everyone understands, the dedication for something perfect to be made, the harmony of colours, the taste and the smell.

At some point in his life he went to a presentation of a French wine maker from Chile Ms Alexandra Marnier, who called her winery 'Casa Lapostolle'. This woman was a descendant of the Marnier Family, who had made the famous French liqueur Grand Marnier and left France; she bought a couple of suitable extents of land in Chile and, with her husband, set up the vineyards and the winery. All this doesn't have much importance, not as much as one thing he saw in her presentation, which had a huge impact on him.

At the winery, when the grapes would come in, the separation of the bunches for a specific kind of wine took place by hand – by many workers. Even after the development, the big steps man had taken forward in technology, during the twentieth century, somewhere in Chile and perhaps in other areas of the world, those who wanted to stand out, made wine using conventional methods; simple, old, traditional methods, a return to manual work.

From that day on, Yiannis started writing his thoughts by hand and, after transferring them to the computer, he started studying them a little better. For them to make better wine, instead of separating the grapes from the bunches in a much faster manner, they used the traditional method. And Yiannis took his pen and wrote, and he always kept his handwritten copies. From the moment he wrote with his pen he thought he was living in an era of about a hundred years before and that he contributed in a similar way by writing the story of the world.

But who was he to be thinking in this way? A graphic, romantic, anonymous man who believed in dreams, in good fairies, in his duty to also write some random verses in the book of the history of the world. The world was progressing, but at the same time it was becoming unhappy. People raised money, because society and government had failed to look after everyone, people created hospices and other private institutions, because governments had failed in the work of social welfare.

Just like they separated the grapes by hand, he wrote with his pen and the world perhaps had to start seeking for happiness in smaller simpler things that cost nothing.

A walk on the beach, a smile, more use of the word 'we', suppression of the word 'I', and the use of more balanced emotions. To talk, but to listen more and to learn, to smell the flowers, to listen to sounds and messages of nature, to seek the peak of mountains, the waves, the tears and our hearts, and each other's hands. To drink wine by stopping everything else around us, just to make us feel the magical taste in our mouths and souls.

Yiannis believed in all of this and he wrote about it with passion. What he wrote was who he was and everything he represented and he gave life to soulless paper with his sixth sense as a guide, his intuition.

Paulina Antinopoulou – Assessment of a Lifetime

Sometimes small children think of the most wise, clever and unbelievable things. In their home, when their children were young, they had a small cage with four little birds. Each one of them had a name relevant to its colour. White tooth, the Yellowish one, the Green-nosed one and the Light-blue-tailed one. The birds lived in their own microcosm, they chirped, ate seeds, drank water, sharpened their beaks and nails, played with each other, sometimes they fought and sometimes they kissed.

One day, as Paulina was cleaning the cage carefully, her young daughter asked her.

"Mum, if we leave the door of the cage open, will the birds fly away?"

Paulina didn't know what to answer. She gave a quick answer that afterwards turned out to be very logical and wise.

"They probably will leave, darling. Their nature will call upon them to free themselves, they will come out, they will fly and they will go away. I think though that things won't turn out to be that easy for them, they won't know how to find water to drink, or any food; they haven't learnt how to do this outside a cage. They might even start flying around their home, near their cage and even, one or two of them may return."

On that same night she thought about that morning's discussion, in bed, next to her husband who was fast asleep. They had made love that night and then, they each did their own thing. He fell asleep peacefully, happy; she stayed awake listening to the existent and non-existent sounds of the night, looking, as she often did, at the ceiling, in between her thoughts and prayers with the sole company of her conscience. From the moment that settles the daily routine and horizontally laying down, you look for solutions and answers to the puzzles of your life.

The birds are in their cage, with food, water and security. They have a safe life in the frames in which they move and if you open up the cage, they will react. There is no wrong and right in what they are doing, everything is relevant.

All the more for humans. Their whole life is full of such roads, dilemmas, crossroads. Their yes's and no's, their black and white, the wrong and right road, the good and bad are imprinted and stigmatised in their life. They can't always find grey areas. They can't always say maybe; at some point they have to take a position, a stand.

'No' is one of the most difficult words for a man to say while they are teenagers, in their youth, in their studies.
 At the time when everybody smokes and they offer you a cigarette, you can say no if you want to. You have to be able to say no to your girlfriend, if she wants to go out every night, when you want a little time to find yourself or your friends. You have to be able to say no to your boyfriend if he insists on making love and you don't feel ready yet. You have to be able to say no to an absurd action that you don't want to do; you have to learn to resist.

On the other hand though, when you 'chill out', when you find your lake, when you have sunk in stagnant waters and every day is the same as the next, you start finding it difficult to say yes. Yes to new political powers that represent you more, yes to changes in life, yes to painting your room in a more modern colour, yes to quick and effective methods of work.

Two small words that can destroy or make us in life.

'Truly,' wondered Paulina, 'could I use these words in a more tragic way?' She smiled melancholically because she knew that her choices were wrong without her being a superficial person. Obviously though she had made big mistakes.

Our 'yes's' and 'no's' follow us throughout our lives. Our happiness in life, in our decisions, it is very much based on our correct judgment and our good judgment is based on the experiences we attain. Our experiences though, on many occasions are results of our bad judgment and of the mistakes we have committed, from which we also learn.

And even though whatever is done cannot be undone, even though time cannot be brought back, even though the theatre of life hasn't got any margins for rehearsal, nevertheless, many times, history repeats itself. Under other circumstances, with other faces, at a different time. Only then can a story end peacefully with its protagonists, good actors now, who follow their 'yes's' and 'no's' in a wiser manner. With logic but also from the heart in proportions that are suitable in each case.

Lying horizontally with her eyes fixed to the ceiling, she thought about all these mistakes, the birds, her children who were anything but a mistake, most probably they were her lighthouse that gave her light and hope, her husband that she loved too, Dionysis whom she loved. She contemplated her dilemmas, her decisions, the future, herself, until everything around her started jumping around and, for a couple of seconds, a passage from the conscious to the subconscious and to the unexplainable world of sleep, she whispered some words without meaning, without cohesion.

Then she lost herself in a kind of wind, softly, and started dreaming of princesses and princes, a beautiful dream. The other dream, the nightmare, the bad dream that was coming for a long time and upset her daily life, seemed to have subsided. Her prince Dionysis had saved her from it.

Dionysis Meletakis – Life with Colour and Hope

Dionysis's heart had crumbled into a thousand pieces two years ago and now he was trying, in beautiful Thessaloniki, to pick the pieces of the puzzle up and put them back together. The puzzle, which even though a while ago had an image of a dull deserted landscape, now started to return and find its colours. Lying in bed he looked at the beautiful firm and well-shaped body of the girl who was sleeping on his chest with warmth, while he, a little higher up, was leaning on his pillow.

He brought the puzzle to mind and was trying to put an order in things. His mind went to the women who had marked his life. His mother who had brought him into this world, whom he never enjoyed or remembered, but with whom he had had so many nice conversations.

The girl in high school, the first great love he had practically no response from. Cleo, his wife with whom he shared so much, they had two wonderful children, they built a life together, even though everything in the end was left in mid-air.

Then came Paulina, his secret, his sin but his blessing also, the reason why he found himself where he was now. I wonder, did they all have a common denominator that escaped him, or didn't he notice? Was there something that connected them with him? As much as he tried, he never managed to answer this question.

He had met Rena on one of his nights out. In the beginning he avoided these things, he had one or two flirts that didn't lead anywhere. Maybe he sought for these failures and of course, made himself clear from the beginning. He didn't lie, he didn't flatter. Perhaps this is also something Rena saw in him, and she appreciated him. A very successful architect, a career woman, around her thirties, quite a bit younger than him, who knew very well what she wanted. One of these things was a more open relationship, anything but suffocating.

She had been engaged young but separated, she loved her work, she was a good person; they were a match made in heaven. You may say that under such circumstances, you don't say I want this and that and everything works like clockwork. Many times, the balances are fine, persistent effort is necessary for a relationship to be harmonious, and as you have imagined it to be. Aren't all relationships supposed to be like this though? Aren't marriages the same too? Isn't everything based on mutual understanding, harmony and balance?

'Things worked out quite well,' Dionysis thought, while caressing Rena's hair; she seemed to enjoy it in her sleep and he continued roaming in between the ruins of the puzzle. Is the word 'ruins' harsh? Some roads had cleared. He looked on the other side of things too, there where all the males in his circle were. His father, Father Ieroclis, Costas his friend, his boys and the anonymous friend, the writer who accompanied him in a deep confession at the Monastery of the Fools.

'I wonder what he's up to, where he is, has he found his way? If he writes something one day and becomes famous will I get to know about it? I'll surely become the most fanatic reader, whatever he publishes. It's the first time in my life that a person listened to me so carefully, with so much interest. Will we be able to shake hands, to embrace, have a coffee together and get to know each other? One day perhaps... but talking about confession...how is Father Ieroclis...?'

Yes, in the end there aren't ruins all over the place. The white, the black and the grey of the puzzle of the heart and of Dionysis's life had started gaining some additional colour, roads started clearing. The paths didn't only have thorns, but greenery and flowers and jasmine and cyclamen.

'Yes, yes, cyclamen,' he thought and his mind travelled to Mount Athos, which was one of his first missions when he had arrived in Thessaloniki.

His children were growing up, the bridges between them gradually were being rebuilt on more stable grounds. Cleo had, in the beginning, comported herself with quite a lot of malice, more so from egoism, but she brought her children up well and she never said anything bad about their father in front of them.

Rena opened her eyes, looked at him and smiled.

"What is it, again you travelling prince? Can I come with you too?"

They smiled to each other. He didn't answer. Even though she teased him often about the fact that he got lost in his own world so often, she didn't mean any harm. On the contrary, it had become his 'thing' and his friends and colleagues in Thessaloniki teased him about it and had also given him a nickname. They called him 'master' and 'guru' because sometimes, even though they were all together, he travelled to other places. He counted his life, he lived on other spiritual levels, maybe he didn't chase after mirages but after 'the Paulina's' in his life. This last part he never told anyone about. Only sometimes did he think, if he really had been a guru in another life.

Hindus say that man, the soul, lives many lives and every time it becomes better. The ultimate aim is 'nirvana', completion, perfection. Anyhow, Hinduism believes in reincarnation. He believed that the soul did live forever, it never dies, it exists. He wasn't sure if we met the same soul in other people though. He felt that the soul is really unique, special and different for each person. Its identity, its passport for the over or underworld, for paradise, for completion.

What confused him though, was that certain people he knew, put his father as the first and best example, a man who was almost uneducated academically, from a village, hosted such a polite, superior soul. They were so wise, so rich internally that, as much as they had been taught from their grandfathers, grandmothers, their circle of friends, they were always a little bit ahead in their wisdom. And what tormented him was that there were people who found themselves on a higher level than others. Surely they must have previously gone through many other stages, other lives perhaps, in which they became better. This caused confusion to him because he didn't want to believe in reincarnation.

He thought of himself as a Hindu in meditation, a guru locked in a cave, who could remain in the same spot for many days without food and water, he could heal sick people with his touch, and the power of his thoughts. He smiled...

Rena helped him settle into his flat, to start to care for certain things, such as the theatre and painting exhibitions. He also took her on outings to different places, wherever the road took them. She would tell him that she had a thousand and one things to do and that she couldn't follow him everywhere because she didn't have the time. He answered that, once upon a time he had also thought like that, but that this tactic was wrong.

"When you have a clear mind, you can do what you want better and more effectively. And you have to live the present vividly and enjoy everything, even the least important things, the most beautiful things in life don't cost anything."

In the end he would convince her and they would go out to the country and when the stress subsided, they both attained a more humane face. That was when the time really stopped and they enjoyed everything around them. That, which most people allow to go by unnoticed because they are blindfolded and carry their balance on a daily basis without knowing where they are going.

No, no, the puzzle of Dionysis's life was correcting itself, it was gaining meaning, colour and hope. It was filling up with flowers and fragrances, he was smiling at life again...

CONCLUSION

Adoration

At the same time, from all corners of an island, many people start heading towards the Monastery of the Fools. Each of them has his or her own story and goes there for their own reasons. They are all tied together by a huge human need. Ultimately, the need of reconciliation with their selves.

A father who sets off from afar to go and find his daughter, Nun Ilaria, in order to ask her for forgiveness. He hears about her from so many people who have found their peace and comfort in her words and he, from cowardness and stubbornness, denied his child for so many years.

Solutions are always given by God. Only he with the humble form of our conscience can tell us something and we can listen.

Paulina is driving towards the monastery and has brought her children along too. She wants them to get acquainted with the place that stood as a home to her throughout her difficult years, for them to meet Father Ieroclis who relieved her since he listened to her secrets and shared her drama.

Paulina, how many Paulina's are there, not only on the little island but in the whole world. In India, in Africa, in the Middle East, in the western world. Women who undertook the weight of the world at such a young age, at such a tender age. Women who, either because they were compelled from habits and their parents, or because they went into a marriage to escape from the oppressive establishment of their home, suddenly lost their innocence, just like the sun disappears behind the mountains. One moment they all smiled carefree, and the other, the sky darkened, dusk came. One moment they saw their firm breast in the mirror and a sweet pleasure conquered, the next moment they were breastfeeding an innocent child.

'Is that bad?' 'Not at all,' but in most cases, the end of the play brings along storms and rain. Broken homes. And in homes where they haven't formally dissolved, living together becomes even more horrible. Two strangers cohabit under the same roof and agree tactfully to satisfy perhaps, on some occasions, their sexual needs, in order to defuse in this way, the stress of everyday life. Sometimes you may hear a 'my love' at the peak, in the paroxysm before the abyss and the dark.

Paulina had fallen into this maelstrom, responsible to a great extent, since she had pushed her fate a little too much. An oxymoron really, a vicious circle in which everyone wants to learn how to run before they learn how to walk, and in which perhaps only a few succeed.

She had fought this, she was a wonderful wife and mother, she looked after her home, she knew where to draw the line, everyone saw her as a prototype until the woman in her betrayed her. She gave herself to a fraud, a sediment of society, and she fell madly in love, with passion, with a great man, Dionysis. She ephemerally felt orgasms of the body, but she felt more intensely the orgasms of the soul and this is precisely what made her pick herself up in the end, to save herself, to discover Paulina.

Yiannis is going there with Erato. He wants to show her the place where the drama took place on one summer afternoon. Then, when he was driving his old car, he followed a sign of a more difficult and narrow road which, in the end, wrote *success*. Is it the end that counts? Perhaps not, but, the end target was the aim for which he gave himself in body and soul. If you don't have a specific goal, if you don't know where you are going then you will end up somewhere else. His "Ithaca" though, offered him the beautiful trip, and now he had understood well, or better put, he had experienced what Ithacas actually meant.

A mythical Odysseus, a few thousands of years ago, was looking for his motherland, Ithaca for ten whole years. A lonely pessimist and a tremendously well-dowered poet, Kavafis, used Ithaca allegorically about the walk of our lives. The walk of Yiannis's life wasn't over, indeed his course with Erato had only now begun. He had also gone on a trip during the past few years. He believed and followed his dreams; he met Dionysis and the universe conspired for the miracle. He was now going, with the partner of his life, to exchange vows at the monastery of miracles, just like Alice in Wonderland, like a dream.

Costas, a mere observer, was driving towards the monastery where the lives of so many people were shaped. As was his friend's, Dionysis, he whom he helped when he wanted to start afresh. He saw Paulina once a year for five consecutive years before he had spoken to her and then they became friends. And he also helped her. In the end, Costas felt as though he had got back twice as much as he had given. He learnt so much, changed some of his ideals, became wiser, met Sister Ilaria and listened to her, he sought inside of him, he realised many truths about himself, his wife, his children, his upbringing, the upbringing that he had to give to his children.

It's worth referring also to other protagonists of our story, who played smaller roles. Alkis, Yiannis's brother, who got lost in the crowd of a big city, he became an anonymous happy man who made his decisions the sooner he could in order to not be tormented. His parents, the people of the system, conservative that is, without them even realising how, had two children who both became revolutionists and not slaves; they looked within themselves, went through rough things and found happiness. They were happy with their children and with what they knew, but also perhaps, with many other things that they didn't know.

Pauline was always there. In the end she also accomplished her dream. She left the public health sector, she also left London and returned to Bath, from where she originally came. A small quiet town with a huge history and wonderful Georgian as well as Victorian buildings. A town that took its name from the Roman baths, the baths that still exist there.

A couple of thousands of years ago, Romans had pools, heated baths, rooms with steam; they created warmness and relaxation. They had no reason to be jealous of contemporary jacuzzis and saunas.

And so she returned to Bath, a smaller place and perhaps more humane. London had tired her out. She returned with her husband with whom she had been sharing her life for the past ten years, Kieran. They lived their dream by opening a small home for old people. Both of them had been in the health sector all their lives, they were doing something relevant with the job they both loved. And at some point, after so many years of happy communal living, they got married. They made official what they had had for so many years by having a beautiful wedding in their sixties, with about seventy guests, amongst whom, guess who was invited, Ms Orthodoxia, Paulina, her daughter, Sophia, three different generations with one thing in common. Their dedication to certain people, to certain important moments that people share all around the world, just like the magic of eternal connection.

Cleo, Dionysis's first wife, a woman of magazines and cosmic life. Honest and moral, but mentally tired from the 'hole' in which she had been trapped for many years. She had drifted into the currents of the good life, the demands of high society. She liked being the big fish in the pond. Her small island suited her; that was the world which she considered perfect.

Dionysis had made her life difficult, he had embittered her. But in the end, then when the war took place, then, when they exchanged, perhaps, harsh words, then, when hate overloaded and the bitterness of the glass of a conventional relationship, Cleo started to see things clearer. And she became a better person for herself above all, but also, for her children and her new partner.

I wonder if the completion of love, the beautiful, peaceful, absolute relationship, as all things, is a true Odysseus that perfects itself with experience. Yes, perhaps our soulmate exists, but maybe there isn't just one. Maybe the meeting of soulmates also has to do with timing and the right context. Two people at the right time let out the golden side of themselves, or get rid of their bad side and, utterly healthy now, they let out and give out everything for each other's soul.

Before the curtain closes indefinitely, Dionysis, our protagonist, also enters the stage,. The man who was faithful to his virtues and his friends. The man who wrote this story. He didn't seek it, many things happened because they were going to happen anyhow. But he made sure to make wiser decisions on his way.

Some often say: 'Why is God unfair, why doesn't he do this, why doesn't he do that?' or at other times 'since there is a God why are there wars, poor people, death, evil?' Because God made man with a brain and judgment and man has the responsibility for his decisions. And Dionysis took them and paid quite a bit for them too...

He came to Cyprus; started from scratch with his admonition and blessed conceivable advices of his mother as his only supplies. He worked hard, got married, built a family, had two boys to whom he gave everything. He continued working, he had the touch of Midas; whatever he touched turned into gold. And this bothered some people who went out to destroy him without them knowing that, in the end, other roads would open up for him, roads hard to cross, but full of knowledge and love.

He reached his limits and there he found out how good he was and how much power he had. He was forced out of his shell and discovered other places, other people, other dimensions to his feelings and in his life. Then, when he was falling, he got up, he wanted to live. Until slowly things got quiet, he quenched his thirst, he found himself, became a better person and moved on...

Did we forget anyone? Yes, Father Ieroclis, Dionysis's father, and maybe others'. All these people were part of the performance, they participated in the play. Because what else is life, than a play, a game in which at some point we win, some other times we lose but always, we learn. Every Dionysis, every Paulina, every Yiannis, consists of a type of person that is in danger of extinction. That's why I chose to speak about these people, because they are worth dealing with for a while, for us and others, the many, the crowd that got lost in the 'musts' and on many occasions don't dare to live....

To end, when the curtain will close and the lights will go out, each of us will make our own assessment....

And so, they travel from different parts of the island, all these heroes, towards the Monastery of the Fools. On the spot some chapters will close and others will open.

Everything flows, nothing stops, everyone moves along with the rhythm of time. The seconds, the hours, the days, the years, the centuries, all have dimensions. The monastery stands there serene; it has opened its arms on a beautiful afternoon in September and awaits them. The lemon blossoms smell beautifully, the smell of jasmine, the concert that the crickets put on at the end.

The bell for the afternoon mass rings, the nuns move up and down as if they know that today something different is about to happen. The candles light up, in and around the church where there are candelabra. The paved slabs. Nature is happy and an incredible peace spreads in and out of the monastery.

A cloud covers the monastery like a nimbus, like the flame of the candles that covers and protects with warmth. And there, at the exit of the monastery, on a huge column, which looks like it used to be a bell tower in the past, he sits there; the sleepless guard of the Monastery of the Fools. He who protects the monastery from evil, for centuries now, but also all the bad of this world. A huge eagle with an aristocratic stature and a sad eagle's glance.

In the small church, two people who have passed their forties, Dionysis and Paulina, hold hands and embrace quietly. Words are not needed. The communication between them all these years never ceased to exist. Simply now, they can lean on each other and, if they choose to, they can decide to move on together in the avenue of life that has opened up in front of them.

They have grown up, they have their children as bright lighthouses in their course, but they have managed to remain children themselves, because they made sure to leave behind a small golden piece of their soul completely intact. Now walked on, like fresh snow, innocent like the heart of a sparrow, peaceful like the smile of Sister Ilaria.

Yes, if they choose to. Because, while in fairy tales, at this point, marriage always takes place, in a ceremony which lasts for three days and three nights, and they live happily ever after, here a story full of storms has already been written. Two people fought in the open seas with the waves; the storm separated them, but the good dolphin led them, first the one and then the other, to different harbours, safe, and at the right time it brought them back together again, in a small quiet harbour named love.

They are not alone. Their kids are all grown up, they have their career, they have separate lives. They got hit many times, they endured and carried on and created their new world that cannot change that easily again….

On the other hand though, as Paul the Apostle wrote in his letter to the Corinthians:

'…*love will never cease to exist. The holy messages of our ancestors, one day, will not exist anymore, linguistics will cease, the knowledge of Holy messages will stop. Because our knowledge and our prophecies only limit us in one part of the truth. But when the perfection that we await for will arrive, then only the partial will stop to exist…*

...now I only know one part, then I will know with plenitude, just as God had gotten to know me.

In the end, the three values in life will always remain: faith, hope and love. And from these, the greatest one is love.'